SUNNY DAYS INSIDE
AND OTHER STORIES

SUNNY DAYS INSIDE
and Other Stories

Caroline Adderson

Groundwood Books
House of Anansi Press
Toronto / Berkeley

Published in 2021 by Groundwood Books / House of Anansi Press
groundwoodbooks.com

Groundwood Books respectfully acknowledges that the land on which we operate is
the Traditional Territory of many Nations, including the Anishinabeg, the Wendat and
the Haudenosaunee. It is also the Treaty Lands of the Mississaugas of the Credit.

We gratefully acknowledge for their financial support of our publishing
program the Canada Council for the Arts, the Ontario Arts Council and
the Government of Canada.

 Canada Council
for the Arts **Conseil des Arts**
du Canada **ONTARIO ARTS COUNCIL**
CONSEIL DES ARTS DE L'ONTARIO
an Ontario government agency
un organisme du gouvernement de l'Ontario

With the participation of the Government of Canada
Avec la participation du gouvernement du Canada | Canadä

Library and Archives Canada Cataloguing in Publication
Title: Sunny days inside and other stories / Caroline Adderson.
Names: Adderson, Caroline, author.
Identifiers: Canadiana (print) 20200393642 | Canadiana (ebook) 20200393677
| ISBN 9781773065724 (hardcover) | ISBN 9781773065731 (EPUB) |
ISBN 9781773065748 (Kindle)
Subjects: LCGFT: Short stories.
Classification: LCC PS8551.D3267 S86 2021 | DDC jC813/.54—dc23

Jacket illustration and design by Claudia Dávila
Text design and typesetting by Marijke Friesen
Printed and bound in Canada

Groundwood Books is a Global Certified Accessible™ (GCA by Benetech) publisher.
An ebook version of this book that meets stringent accessibility standards is available
to students and readers with print disabilities.

Groundwood Books is committed to protecting our natural environment.
This book is made of materials from well-managed FSC®-certified forests,
recycled material and other controlled sources.

For Danika and Ryker
and all the children of the pandemic

CONTENTS

1

APARTMENT
4A

Sunny Days Inside

We were supposed to go on holiday, but we didn't. We stayed home.

By holiday I mean an *airplane* holiday, not a *car* holiday with me stuck in the back with Mimi in her booster seat with the cup holders full of guck. (Guck = crumbs and dirt and tissue lint glued on with dried apple juice, which gives me car sickness *x 10*.)

We were all disappointed, but Mom was disappointed *x 100* because first: she hadn't had an airplane holiday since Before Me (eleven years) because she and Dad are saving money so we can buy a town house and not have to squash together in an apartment.

And second: Auntie Susie, Mom's older sister who lives in an apartment bigger than ours though she's just one person (except it's called a condo because she owns it) takes airplane holidays all the time.

After Mom, I was the second-most disappointed. Then Dad, who just "goes with it." Then Mimi, who was excited about the trip, but worried about Gingersnap.

Gingersnap was the only one who wasn't disappointed at all because he's a cat.

This is how we almost had a real airplane holiday to a real holiday place (= a resort). Grandma gave us the money.

This is Top Secret *x 1,000*. We're not allowed to tell anybody, especially not Auntie Susie.

Grandma is the one who said not to tell Auntie Susie because she (A.S.) might think it was favoritism. (Favoritism = doing something nice for somebody, but not somebody else because you like them better, which is just normal in my opinion. Why would you do nice things for somebody you *don't* like?)

Mom says Grandma loves her and Susie exactly the same amount. She says if you took two measuring cups and filled one with how much Grandma loved Susie and another with how much she loved my mom, the amount would be exactly the same.

"The same way that if I had a Danila (me) measuring cup and a Mimi measuring cup, they would contain exactly the same amount of love," Mom explained.

It was just that if the cups showed how much *money* Auntie Susie had and how much money we have, the measurement wouldn't be the same. Way different! So Grandma topped up our cup.

(Shhhhhh …)

"Can we use it for our down payment?" Dad asked when he found out about the money. (Down payment = the money you need to save up before they'll sell you a town house.)

"No," Mom said, and she crossed her arms over her chest and looked at him with the Laser Zapper Eyes that we're all scared of though mostly it's Dad who gets zapped.

"I'll go with it."

He uncrossed Mom's arms and hugged her until Mimi saw them and shouted, "Mimi sandwich!" and ran over and wriggled between them.

Mimi is seven and can never get enough love. She even smears yogurt on her lips and lets Gingersnap lick it off, which is disgusting. *Coffee* yogurt (disgusting *x 10*). What kid eats *that*? What *cat*?

Planning the airplane holiday was probably almost as fun as the airplane holiday would have been.

First we ordered the brochures online. Now there was something to look forward to when we collected the mail! In fact, Mimi and I had never even used that cute little key that opens the box.

When Mom picked us up from school, she brought the key. The first thing we did when we got to our apartment building was race each other to the mailbox. Whoever reached it first opened the box, which was 99.9 percent of the time me because my legs are twice as long. Even though I let Mimi use the key to lock the empty box afterward (which I thought was more than fair), she started baby-bawling so we had to take turns.

If there was a brochure in the mail, we ran up all three flights of stairs to our apartment so we could start living the dream. The pages looked good and felt good — shiny and smooth. Cool, even though the pictures were of hot places. They even *smelled* good, all inky and papery. If we left the brochures on the sofa, Gingersnap would stretch out on them like the bikini women inside sunning themselves on the beach.

We ordered brochures for airplane holidays all over the world even though we knew we'd never pick Bermuda (too expensive), or Costa Brava, Spain (too far *and* too expensive), or the Galapagos Islands (too far and too expensive *and* too prickly with cacti and creepy spiky lizards). We just wanted to look at the pictures and smell the paper.

•

One weekend Auntie Susie dropped by. We weren't even dressed yet, but she looked ironed. She'd already been to the gym and the mall. She brought presents — a sparkly pen and notebook for me and another Polly Pocket for Mimi. (Sometimes Mom gets annoyed by all the presents Auntie Susie buys us.)

Auntie Susie saw Gingersnap sunning himself on his brochure beach and pulled one out from under him.

"Going somewhere?"

"We're going on an airplane holiday!" Mimi shouted.

Then she started doing a hula dance like in the Hawaii brochures, singing, "Airplane holiday, airplane holiday ..."

Mom brought Auntie Susie a cup of coffee.

Auntie Susie said, "I thought you didn't have any disposable income."

"*Disposable* income?" I said. "Is that like *throwing money away*?"

"Is it like *diapers*?" Mimi asked, cracking up.

Mom told Auntie Susie, "You have to have a little fun sometimes, right? Who knows what the future might bring?"

Auntie Susie's face squinched, her eyes, nose and mouth bunching all together. "Where are you thinking of going?"

"Not sure yet." Mom seemed nervous, or afraid Auntie Susie might tickle-torture it out of her that the money wasn't disposable. It was Grandma's.

(Auntie Susie used to tickle-torture Mom when they were the same age as me and Mimi. She was *merciless x 100*.)

But Auntie Susie wasn't interested in the money. She said, "Maybe we could go somewhere together. All of us."

Mom said, "Maybe," in a voice that sounded like somebody was squeezing her throat. Hard. Then she asked, "How's your coffee?"

The embarrassing moment would have passed, except Mimi stopped hula-ing.

"*Can* Auntie Susie come with us?" she asked.

"We'll see." Mom went to get the coffee pot even though Auntie Susie's mug was still full.

Auntie Susie sat for a minute without saying anything. Then she sniffed.

"It always smells so weird in here," she said. "Like cat litter and peanut butter."

"Then smell this!" Mimi grabbed a brochure and fanned the pages in her face.

In the end we chose the resort by price. Días de Sol Resorts — children under 10 half price! — in Baja, Mexico. (Días de Sol = Sunny Days.) We checked the reviews to make sure there weren't cockroaches, sharks, or prickles.

Not only was the resort right on the ocean, there was also a swimming pool. A swimming pool *and* the ocean! How great was that?

We didn't invite Auntie Susie.

"It won't be up to her standards," Mom said at dinner that night.

"She'll think it smells weird," I said.

Everybody laughed, but I felt bad as soon as I said it. Because I remembered how Auntie Susie had looked down into her coffee mug when Mom wouldn't answer her question about coming on the trip with us. She hadn't taken a sip yet, but it was like she saw an empty cup.

•

About a month before we were supposed to leave, we went shopping for "resort wear." (Resort wear = sundresses, sunglasses, sun hats, sun flip-flops ...) Mom and Dad could just wear their summer clothes, but Mimi and I had grown out of ours.

Since there weren't any summer clothes in the stores, we went to the Thrift Store and tried on outfits and pretended to be fashion models strutting the aisles. We came home with a whole bag of crazy resort wear that cost practically nothing, leaving us more money to dispose of (= spend) when we were actually at the resort. Not only was this cheaper than new clothes, but when I wore the T-shirt that said *I HEART Miami*, or *California Dreamin'*, people at the resort would think I'd actually been there.

A few weeks before we were supposed to leave, Mimi and I started to practice packing because we were only allowed carry-on bags. You had to pay for a bigger bag, so we had to figure out how to fit everything in.

Mimi's bag bulged. She was planning on bringing her blanket! Also her whole Polly Pocket collection!

"No, no, no," I told her, pulling stuff out.

She started yelling for me to stop.

"You want to leave room to bring things back, don't you?" I told her. "Like souvenirs and a present for Grandma and Auntie Susie."

"I have to buy presents?"

"Duh! Auntie Susie has bought you about a thousand presents, and Grandma gave you this trip."

"What about Gingersnap?" she asked.

"Sure," I told her. "Bring him a present, too."

"He's coming, isn't he? In his carrier?"

I'm not sure if she really thought we were taking him or she was in denial. Once we did take him on a car trip after he scratched Grandma and she wouldn't look after him anymore. That trip was a disaster *x 1,000*. Gingersnap howled in the car. Then he howled all night in the motel. We went home the next morning.

I gave it to her straight. "Gingersnap's not coming."

Mimi ran off crying to Mom and Dad, who confirmed the awful truth. Juliet from next door was going to feed him and change his litter box.

All the baby-bawling about Gingersnap was interrupted then by the phone. It was Grandma calling to say that Auntie Susie was leaving on her cruise soon and maybe Mom could phone her and wish her bon voyage.

"What cruise?" Mom said. She hadn't spoken to Auntie Susie since that day she visited and said our apartment smelled weird.

"What's a cruise?" Mimi asked.

"It's like what we're doing, but on a ship," I told her.

"And way fancier," Dad said.

He told us about all the things a cruise ship had. Swimming pools (more than one!), game arcades, movie theaters, restaurants and discos.

It sounded fantastic *x 10,000*.

Later, though not in front of us — after we all went to bed, but before I fell asleep — Mom complained to Dad about Auntie Susie's cruise. This is one of the problems when you're squashed together in an apartment. You can hear everything on the other side of the wall — even things you'd rather not hear — especially if your bed is the one next to the wall.

"My whole life I've had to deal with this sibling-rivalry thing. She always has to be better than me."

"Maybe she just wants to be good enough for you," Dad said.

"Hardly! I hope Danila and Mimi don't end up like this."

What did *that* mean? I *am* three years older than Mimi like Auntie Susie is three years older than Mom, but I'm not like her at all. I've never tickle-tortured Mimi. I'm pretty much a perfect older sister.

The next day we called Auntie Susie and shouted, "Bon voyage!"

Then Mimi grabbed the phone. "Is it true there's two swimming pools on your ship?"

And that's the problem with sibling rivalry. Before we found out about the arcade and the movie theater and all the other amazing things on the cruise ship, we were thrilled about our resort.

Now it didn't seem that great.

•

Three days before we were supposed to leave on the airplane there was more Bedroom Talking. "Is it safe?" "It's safe now, but when won't it be safe?" "It's not actually bad here." "It's not bad there either." "What about the

19

money?" "But what about the kids? They'll be so disappointed." "Should we go?" "If it's safe, we should."

I pressed my ear so hard against the wall it hurt.

"What are they talking about?" Mimi asked from her bed.

"Nothing, nosy."

She jumped across the space and put her bedhead to the wall.

"Get out of my territory," I told her. When she didn't leave, I said I'd snake-bite her arm. She squeaked and got out fast.

Mom and Dad must have heard us because they stopped talking after that.

In the morning Mom took us to school smiling so hard *my* teeth hurt. She didn't say anything about the trip or what they were worried about.

I found out the second part at school because some of the kids were talking about the virus. It couldn't have been that bad, I thought, because it seemed as though we were going away after all, and so were a lot of other kids.

That night, Mom and Dad came into our rooms to check that we had packed everything we needed. Mimi's suitcase was bulging again even though she'd taken out everything I'd asked her to take out.

Dad lifted my suitcase off the bed to test its weight. They make you pay extra if it's too heavy.

"Oof," he said, pretending it weighed a ton. Then he lifted Mimi's.

"MEOW!" came from inside.

•

The last day of school, all the kids were bouncing off the walls. Spring break!

We're going on an airplane trip! We're going on an airplane trip! I sang under my breath all day.

And then we weren't. As fast as that, everything changed.

We were staying home instead.

Dad had been worried about disappointing me and Mimi, and we *were* disappointed *x 10.* But, as I said, Mom was disappointed *x 100.* She went to her room and closed the door. We could hear her crying the way she cried in a sad movie — big loud sobs and honks when she stopped to blow her nose.

Mimi asked through the door, "Mommy? Can I come in and hug you?"

Mom croaked, "No, sweetheart. Not yet."

So Mimi spread out her blanket and lay in front of the door. I lay beside her.

"Is she crying because of the virus?" Mimi whispered. She must have heard about it at school, too.

"Sort of," I said.

"What's a virus?"

I told her it was a sickness, but I didn't completely understand yet. Because a cold is a virus. And all that barfing at Christmas was because of a virus.

"Is that why Mom doesn't want a hug?" Mimi asked.

"No. She just wants to be alone for a little while."

"But they said no hugs at school."

"You can still hug people in your family."

"Oh, good," Mimi said.

I moved away from her on the blanket in case she decided to hug me. She's like Velcro. You have to rip her off.

Dad was over at the desk in the corner of the living room doing something on the computer. A big smile spread across his face.

Careful not to step on us, he came over and said through the door, "Great news, Debbie! It's refundable!"

He grinned and gave us the thumbs-up.

Something smashed hard against the door. Maybe a shoe? Mimi shrieked and we both sat up.

"It's not about the money!" Mom yelled. "Do you have any idea how tired I am? How much I needed that trip? Of course Susie gets hers, like she always does! A break! I just wanted a break! To lie in the sun and DO NOTHING for a change!"

I expected two laser holes to burn through the door.

Dad felt terrible then, I could tell. He pressed his forehead to the door. "I'm sorry, Deb. What can I do to help?"

The yelling scared Gingersnap. He ran off to hide and some of the brochures slid off the couch and onto the floor. I looked over at them.

Mom just wanted a break.

We can give her a break, I thought. A break *x 10*. Maybe even *x 100*.

I pulled Dad's pant leg to get him to crouch down. I whispered my idea in his ear.

•

While Dad was at the store, Mimi and I got everything ready. After we changed into our resort wear, we got to work pushing aside the furniture so there would be room to lay out our towels on the floor. We gathered all the lamps in the apartment and put them up high so they would shine down on the towels like the bright Mexican sun. We turned up the heat.

Dad brought home bags of groceries: tortillas, refried beans, avocados, salsa, chili powder, sour cream. Orange juice and a pineapple to make some fruity drinks. He downloaded some happy Mexican music called mariachi that we listened to while we cooked and danced around wiggling our hips.

We even put up some streamers that we found — green and orange, two of the colors of the Mexican flag — and taped beach pictures torn out of the brochures all over the walls.

Then we knocked on the bedroom door.

Mom must have known we were up to something, but she pretended to be surprised when we said, *"Hola Señora. Bienvenida a nuestro complejo de apartamentos!"* which Google Translate taught us how to say.

We ate enchiladas for dinner, then lay on the beach.

Mom's phone rang and I went and got it for her.

"It's Auntie Susie," I said.

"Turn it off," Mom said. "We're in Mexico."

"Smart," Dad said. "We don't want roaming charges."

Dad cleaned up. He cleaned up every night while we were at the apartment resort, which was just the weekend instead of the whole week. We all cooked (except for Mom, who wasn't allowed to help). All Mom did for the whole holiday was relax and sip her fruity drinks and read her book. We tried to sprinkle in Spanish words when we talked.

"*Buenas noches,* everybody! See you *mañana*!"

"*Está soleado.*"

"Yeah. *Qué calor.*"

On Sunday night, our last night at the resort, we filled the bathtub and put tea lights all around the bathroom. It looked so pretty. You couldn't even see the black around the tiles that won't scrub off. Dad found some ocean sounds and played them on his phone. Then we sat in a row along the edge of the tub and soaked our feet in the Sea of Cortez.

"The stars are amazing," Mom said.

"*Las estrellas,*" Dad said.

"They seem so much closer in Mexico."

Dad kicked his foot. "Did you see that? A *delfín*!"

"Really?" Mimi said.

He kicked again and she cried, "I saw it! I saw it!"

Mom sighed with happiness. She put an arm around me and Mimi and kissed the top of our heads. "*Gracias, chicas.* This is the best holiday I've ever had."

"Better than the airplane holiday?" Mimi asked.

"Yes," Mom said. "All I really want is for us to be together, safe and healthy."

"Then it *is* better than the airplane holiday," Mimi said, "because Gingersnap got to come with us!"

•

I believed Mom when she said our apartment holiday was the best holiday ever. But I don't believe she thought it was better than an airplane holiday. After all, it was make-believe. That's why she didn't want to talk to Auntie Susie — because it would have reminded her about sibling rivalry. That Auntie Susie was on a cruise while we stayed home.

It would have broken the spell.

So it wasn't until after we pushed all the furniture back to where it used to be and threw our beach towels and resort wear into the laundry hamper, after we ripped down the streamers and went back to macaroni and cheese (which tasted soooo good after all those beans), that Mom turned her phone back on.

Then she saw how many missed calls and voice mails there were from Auntie Susie, and also from Grandma.

First she tried to call Auntie Susie.

"Why isn't she answering?" Mom said.

Dad said, "She's probably somewhere out of range. No service —"

Mom called Grandma. "What's going on? What? No! Call me as soon as you hear from her."

Mom hung up and started pacing back and forth across the living room that had been our relaxing beach all weekend. She wasn't relaxed anymore.

"What's going on?" I asked.

"There's been an outbreak on Auntie Susie's ship."

Mom's phone rang. "Susie! Are you okay? Oh, sweetheart! We're on it. We'll get you home! Hang in there. First we need the information. I'm passing you over to Guy."

She handed Dad the phone. He began writing down what Auntie Susie was telling him. She was half-yelling, sounding really scared.

Dad got on the computer to look things up, while Mom tried to calm Auntie Susie. She took the phone to the bedroom and closed the door.

Later, Dad explained the situation to us. Some people on the ship had got the virus. Now everybody had to stay in their cabins. When they tried to dock the ship to let everybody off and get medical help for the sick, they were refused. Nobody wanted the virus to spread on shore. Now the cruise ship was floating somewhere in the middle of the ocean, waiting for a safe harbor.

"What if nobody lets them dock?" I asked.

"Will Auntie Susie get sick, too?" Mimi asked.

"We have to hope she doesn't, sweetie."

That night Mimi couldn't sleep. I couldn't either, not with her sighing and squirming and rustling the covers.

"What's the matter?" I asked.

"I'm thirsty."

Normally I wouldn't, but for some reason I got her a glass of water. She took it from me and drank and drank until it was empty. I went back to the bathroom and filled it up again.

"Auntie Susie has food, doesn't she?" Mimi asked when I came back the second time.

"Yes. But she can't leave her room. Somebody puts a tray outside her door."

"She's all alone?"

"Yes."

Mimi whimpered. "Why didn't Auntie Susie come on holiday with us instead?"

"I wish she had. So does Mom."

Then, instead of going back to my bed, I climbed under the covers with my sister and hugged her hard *x 1,000,000*.

2

APARTMENT
2D

How to Be a Cave Family

1. *Don't cut your hair.*

Ivan's was springy, Alek's was straight. For as long as the twins could remember, they'd visited the barbershop once a month.

When they were little, they used to wait on the bench with the barber's basket of toys between them. Now they played a game on their dad's phone, or just goggled at the barber's deadly arsenal: the scissors and razors and the vat of combs soaking in the poisonous disinfectant. They used to think the blue comb liquid was Gatorade that the barber drank at the end of the day!

Usually there were two barbers working. Ivan and Alek liked it best when both were free and they could sit side by side making faces at each other in the mirror.

The barbers would pump the chairs, lifting the twins into the air. Then, with the cold mist from the spray bottle enveloping them, the brothers would close their eyes.

Snip-snip-snip. Snip-snip-snip. The scissor blades tickled.

Lastly, they bowed their heads, baring the back of their necks for the *bzzzzzz*ing fly of the electric clippers.

•

It was just before spring break when Ivan and Alek went with their dad to the barbershop for the last time. They found a sign taped to the door.

DUE TO PHYSICAL DISTANCING
REQUIREMENTS
THE SHOP WILL BE CLOSED
UNTIL FURTHER NOTICE

They walked on for two blocks where there was another barbershop with almost the same sign on the door. They checked out a third before giving up.

When they got home, Ivan and Alek's dad stopped in front of the hall mirror and ran a hand through his hair, which was wiry and thick like Ivan's.

"I'll look like a cave man before too long," he said. "We all will."

Ivan and Alek burst out laughing. Next thing they knew they were tearing around the apartment, scratching under their arms and grunting to each other. Their mom came out of the bedroom and told them to be quiet or they'd wake the baby.

2. *Be afraid of everybody.*

For the first week of spring break, Ivan and Alek ran wild in the playground with the other kids who lived in their apartment building. Some of the parents stood around talking among themselves.

They were talking about the virus and how it was spreading so fast. Some families canceled their holidays. There was a rumor that school wouldn't start again after the break.

The grown-ups talked in whispers so that the kids wouldn't hear. But the kids heard them anyway.

When they chased each other around, the one formerly known as It was now the "Grown-up Virus," a name one of them had misheard from the whispering grown-ups. "Grown-up Virus" was the last game they played as a group.

The next day, somebody wrapped yellow tape across the entrance to the playground and around the equipment, too. No play dates allowed! You caught the virus from somebody who had it. But not everybody who had it got sick. They might be walking around feeling perfectly normal, infecting everybody with their poisonous invisible spit droplets and maybe even *killing them*.

The safest thing was to *be afraid of everybody*.

Later, when Ivan and Alek did their research, they discovered that this was an actual cave-person trait. Back in the Stone Age, cave people lived in small kin groups. Everybody was related to everybody else. Because resources (all the things you needed to survive, like food, water, firewood and tools) were scarce, you shared everything you had with the group.

But there wasn't enough for people from other kin groups. So if a stranger wandered into your cave, you wouldn't welcome him. You wouldn't offer food and drink. You would assume they were there to kill you so they could take your resources. You'd grab your spear and chase them off.

Anybody could have the virus. If you were out walking and a stranger came along from the opposite direction, one of you had to cross the street.

This was the perfect occasion for the twins to practice their cave-people skills! Ivan would growl in a low voice to alert his cave brother that somebody from an unfamiliar kin group was approaching and probably wanted to kill them with the Grown-up Virus, move into their apartment and eat all the food in their fridge.

Alek would growl back.

Then both boys would bare their teeth and puff out their chests in a threatening manner. If there was a stick or a rock lying on the ground nearby, they'd pick it up and wave it in the air.

At the same time, the oncoming stranger would

notice a cave woman and a cave baby in a stroller along with the two boys. They would immediately cross the street because it would be awkward and dangerous for the cave mom to have to maneuver the stroller up and down the curbs.

The moment the approaching stranger crossed, the cave twins would crow in triumph and run around grunting and scratching under their arms. Underarm scratching meant they were especially pleased about something. (Also, cave people, who were hairy and never bathed, for sure had lice and probably fleas.)

Too bad the cave mom couldn't appreciate how well the cave twins protected their kin group!

"Stop that, you two!" she hissed. "You're embarrassing me!"

3. *Don't go to school.*

The twins' parents were very upset about this. In their home country, their mom was a professor of art history and their dad an information technology specialist. Now that they had immigrated, their dad worked in the IT department of the hospital across the street while their mom stayed home with the baby and supposedly worked on her own art projects.

Even before school was canceled, the cave parents didn't think school was challenging enough. Every evening when the cave dad got home from work, he questioned Ivan and Alek on what they had studied that day and asked to see their homework. Then he would shake his head in disappointment.

Now the teacher was only sending worksheets (later there would be Zoom classes, but they hadn't started yet). When the cave dad got home, he was even less impressed.

"This is ridiculous." He tossed aside the pages that the cave twins had finished in half the time it took them to do the work in school. "They'll be illiterate by the end of all this."

He turned to the cave mom who was trying to quiet the baby. "You've got to tutor them."

"Sure." She deposited the soggy screaming cave baby in his arms and left the room.

Meanwhile, the cave twins started chasing each other around the apartment grunting because it seemed like an illiterate thing to do.

It was the cave dad's night to cook supper. How could he do that with a crying baby and a pair of ten-year-olds running wild?

He would order pizza.

But first the cave dad changed the cave baby and brought her to the cave mom for feeding. He apologized. He said he would get the boys started on a self-directed project where they would research a topic of interest to them and prepare some kind of presentation for the kin group.

The cave twins scratched their underarms in ecstasy. Normally their computer time was strictly limited. Since the libraries were closed, they had no choice but to do their research online.

"How about we research the Stone Age?" Ivan said.

"Excellent," the cave dad replied.

The boys loudly cheer-grunted and got to work.

4. *Hunt and gather.*

Cave people lived around three or four hundred thousand years ago in the Stone Age, which was divided into three distinct periods: the Paleolithic, the Mesolithic and the Neolithic. First they were like apes, but slowly, slowly, they turned into cave people and then, eventually, into Homo sapiens.

Cave people lived in caves, obviously, or sometimes in huts or tepees made out of woolly mammoth skin and tusks. They were hunter-gatherers. That meant they didn't grow their food. Instead they spent all day wandering around searching for berries to pick and animals to kill.

Ivan and Alek went gathering several times a week with their cave mom. In the early days, before their ears were completely covered by their hair, and before leaving the cave was no longer allowed, they would tuck the soccer ball in the bottom of the stroller so that they could stop at the school on the way home and play.

But then they looked up "What are soccer balls made of." No way were polyurethane, latex and polyester available during the Stone Age!

The cave twins didn't go inside the store to help the cave mother gather food. They had to huddle in the corner of the parking lot far away from other kin groups and watch over the cave baby sleeping in the stroller. While they waited — a very long time because of the lineups — they discussed what cave kids must have kicked around instead of a soccer ball.

"Probably a woolly mammoth skull," Alek said.

"That wouldn't roll very far," Ivan said.

But Alek was on the right track. When they looked up "What are soccer balls made of" they learned that the inside of a soccer ball was actually called a bladder.

"We need a bladder," Ivan said, and they both glanced over at the grocery store.

They knew from past visits that all kinds of gross things were sold in the meat department, like pig ears and chicken feet and calf livers. Once Alek had dared Ivan to touch a cow's tongue. The tongue was huge and purple, but Ivan touched it through the plastic wrapping. Then he dared Alek. Just as Alek reached out, Ivan shoved him. Alek's finger punctured the plastic and came into actual contact with the tongue.

It was the worst moment of Alek's life so far.

They ended up kicking a stone around in the parking lot.

"This probably *is* Stone Age soccer," Alek said. "Hunter-gatherers only used stone tools, right?"

The boys pictured the tools they'd seen online: Paleolithic spears and axes.

All at once they came to the same realization, which often happens with twins.

"What are we doing kicking this stone around? We should be *hunting*!"

Between the parking lot and the sidewalk was a row of trees with some patches of dry grass poking through the dirt and stones. They wheeled the stroller over and started filling their pockets with the stones. Some they put in the basket of the stroller to take home.

Cave people hunted animals like woolly mammoth and bison and deer, which were really big. Your aim didn't have to be that good to hit a woolly mammoth. Unfortunately, they were extinct. There weren't any deer or bison wandering in the city either, so Ivan and Alek had to hunt squirrels, which were a lot smaller.

Luckily, there were plenty of them.

The squirrels watched, their eyes bright with curiosity, as the cave twins crept toward them. These squirrels lived beside a busy grocery store, so they weren't afraid of people. Even when the cave twins drew back their arms to hurl the deadly stones, the squirrels didn't bother running. They just blinked at the spot on the ground where the useless stone landed and went on with their own gathering.

Next the cave brothers tried chasing the squirrels, hoping to grab them by their tails. But after a while they got tired.

Alek gave up first. "What would we do if we actually caught one?"

"Kill it and eat it."

"Kill it how?" asked Alek, the sensitive cave twin.

"Duh. With a rock. Then we'd roast it on a stick."

Just then, they heard a bleating sound coming from the stroller. It was the cave baby waking up.

"Hey!" Ivan said. "We could hunt a *baby* no problem!"

Alek was horrified. "But she's in our kin group!"

The cave mom appeared on the other side of the parking lot, pushing a half-empty cart, her scarf wrapped around her nose and mouth.

"The shelves were practically bare," she said when she reached them.

The cave twins helped transfer the groceries into the basket under the stroller. Alek carried the ball.

"Did you see a bladder?" Ivan asked.

"A what?" she asked.

"A bladder. In the meat department."

"We want to make a cave soccer ball," Alek explained.

"If there had been a bladder, I would have bought it and cooked it for lunch. I got the last two cans of tuna."

The hunter-gatherers gave a grunt-cheer. Yay for tuna!

On the way home, they kept an eye out for long sticks lying on the ground. They could use them to make spears after lunch.

5. *Use rudimentary language.*

Nobody knows for sure how cave people talked, but it probably wouldn't have been in full sentences.

If the cave brothers asked their cave dad a question while he was reading the newspaper, he would grunt. The news about the virus was terrible, but he couldn't stop reading. By then his hair was longer than they'd ever seen it, as thick as a scouring pad, just like Ivan's. Alek's straight hair had grown past his ears, while their cave mom now wore hers in a tangled-looking ponytail that nobody had seen her brush recently. The cave baby was still pretty much bald.

The cave dad had also stopped shaving, even though he still went to work every day to gather money. He said all the men at work had stopped shaving out of solidarity with everybody who had been laid off and had no reason to shave.

The cave twins thought there was another reason. Since cave people became Homo sapiens by a long slow process called evolution, there was no reason they couldn't reverse the process and turn from Homo sapiens back into cave people. This was called devolution and was apparently a much faster process. It was practically happening before their eyes! The cave dad was becoming hairier every day and grunting more and more.

As well as grunting, cave people gestured to communicate. But they probably used some words. It would have been too frustrating not to be able to say anything. Ivan and Alek were often frustrated by the limitations of grunting, growling and underarm scratching.

One day when the cave mother was gathering at the grocery store, and after unsuccessfully hunting squirrels, the cave twins got to work writing a cave dictionary. They wrote it in the dirt with a stick because paper and pens didn't exist in the Stone Age. Hardly anything was left behind from the first Stone Age. Just those Paleolithic tools and some cave paintings.

They decided to call the language Ooaw-eek because those were two ape sounds they'd heard on the video they watched. Since they were inventing this language, they named themselves after it. Ivan became Ooaw, leaving Eek for Alek.

ooaw-eek = hello

eek-ooaw = goodbye

oo = yes

aw = no

googoo = cave baby

oogoog = good

moomoo = cave mom

~~poopoo~~ doodoo = cave dad (still hilarious!)

numnum = animal (also food)

This was as far as they got with their cave dictionary when Moomoo called that it was time for numnum.

"Aw!" Ooaw and Eek called back, because they weren't finished inventing words. But Moomoo headed for home pushing the googoo so Ooaw and Eek had to follow.

On the way back from the grocery store, they met a friend from their apartment building. He was out walking his dog.

Ooaw and Eek stopped, confused about what to do

in this situation. Technically, Louis was not in their kin group and neither was Sweet Pea. Also, Sweet Pea was technically a numnum that Ooaw and Eek should kill with stones and roast on a stick.

No way could even Ooaw do that! They loved Sweet Pea!

Clearly, their devolution was not yet complete.

Louis and Sweet Pea crossed to the other side of the street. They all waved to each other and the cave twins shouted, "Ooaw-eek!" Then, "Eek-ooaw!"

After numnums, Ooaw and Eek went out on the balcony to knock stones together. They were making spearheads. It was taking forever to sharpen those stones. No wonder the Stone Age lasted so long!

Moomoo put the googoo down for a nap and came out with her phone to video what they were doing.

"Moomoo, aw!" they yelled, waving her away.

Whoever heard of a Palaeolithic video?

6. *Don't wear clothes.*

It got hot quickly with summer-like weather in the spring. Probably it would cool off again, but for now the cave brothers didn't need coats, or even sweaters.

Inside the cave, they left the door to the balcony and all the windows open. Then they closed them again and turned on the air conditioner, which in Ooaw-eek was a "brrbrr." But the brrbrr wouldn't work and the brrbrr repairer wasn't allowed to come because of the virus.

Cave people wore animal skins around their waists to cover their noonoos. Ooaw and Eek wore underpants while they were in the cave. When they went out to hunt and gather, which they did for hours every day because it was cooler outside (and because Doodoo was working at home now and needed it to be quiet), Moomoo made Ooaw and Eek put on shorts over their underpants.

Eek's hair grazed his shoulders now, and Ooaw's was like a black cloud around his head. Doodoo's, too. Doodoo sat scratching his beard at his desk, wearing his underpants because of the broken brrbrr. And because of devolution.

Moomoo was always videoing their Stone Age activities now. They couldn't stop her. But when she questioned them about what they were doing, they would only grunt or answer in Ooaw-eek.

Moomoo: Why are you banging the rocks together? Is it music?

Ooaw and Eek: Aw.

Moomoo: Aw? What's that?

(Eek shakes his head.)

Moomoo: Ah. Aw is no?

Eek: Oo.

Moomoo: Oo is no, or Aw is? I'm confused. And what are you doing with the rocks?

Ooaw: Numnum! (He grabs a nearby spear shaft and shows her where the spear tip will go when it is finally sharp. He mimes throwing it.)

Moomoo: Ah! You're making a spear?
Ooaw and Eek: Oo.

•

Moomoo played the videos for Doodoo.

"It's their presentation! They've turned it into a performance piece!"

Doodoo sighed and shook his head.

In the basement of the cave — actually in the basement of all the caves, which were stacked one on top of the other — there was a storage room. Moomoo went down at night when she was sure she wouldn't meet somebody from another kin group. She came back with a cardboard box full of art supplies and art books. She showed the brothers pictures of actual cave paintings from the Paleolithic period, of hunters chasing numnums around with spears.

The next day they rearranged Ooaw and Eek's cave, pushing the furniture away from one wall. Moomoo spoke to them in the voice she used with the baby, which was also good to explain things to cave people with rudimentary language. Paints were made from crushed-up stones, she told them. Paleolithic meant "early stone age," and lith meant "stone."

Eek pointed to the pile of stones in the corner. "Lith?"

She nodded. They had a new word for their dictionary!

Then she ran her thumb over the bristles of the paintbrush and said, "Numnum," and pointed to her

43

tangled hair. She was speaking Ooaw-eek to them, assuring them that a paintbrush was made of animal hair, which was a proper Stone Age material. What an oogoog moomoo!

Moomoo put on an old shirt of Doodoo's. The googoo sat in her googoo chair in her diaper, happily gumming a stone that was too big to choke on. She really liked that stone. It was covered in drool. She watched while the rest of her kin group painted the cave.

The Stone Age was here! It was *now*! The deer and bison and woolly mammoth migrated across the wall in Paleolithic colors — ocher and raw umber and burnt sienna — while a nimble kin group of hunters pursued them with spears. Moomoo showed them a picture of another cave where cave artists had placed their hands on the cave wall and painted all around them. Ooaw, Eek and Moomoo painted their hands into the Stone Age scene. Then Moomoo lifted the googoo and placed her tiny hand next to their hand pictures for Eek to trace around.

Doodoo appeared in the doorway with a plastic bag in either hand, his hair like a million flies swarming his head. He must have been out gathering. They'd been so absorbed in their painting, they hadn't even realized he'd left.

"Doodoo?" Eek beckoned for Doodoo to come inside. He placed his own hand on the wall to show him what to do. "Oogoog!"

Doodoo walked off, shaking his cloud of flies.

A few minutes later, the cave artists heard a sound coming from elsewhere in the cave — a sound that was both familiar and not.

Bzzzzzz.

Actual flies?

Ooaw and Eek dropped their paintbrushes and hurried in search of the sound.

They found Doodoo in the bathroom, the door ajar. He was kneeling on the bathmat, his head and shoulders inside the tub like a woolly mammoth drinking at a water hole, a small cardboard box and scattered wrapping paper beside him.

"Bzzbzz?" Eek asked Ooaw, who shrugged.

They came closer to see what was in the water hole. Not water. Not flies either. What they saw was Doodoo's shorn hair piling up.

Doodoo changed the hand that held the electric clippers and began shearing that side of his head. Then he had a go at his chin. When he pulled himself out of the watering hole again, the cave brothers saw standing before them — a Homo sapiens!

What a terrible moment that must have been for the cave people! It was terrible for Ooaw and Eek, too.

"Ivan? Alek?" the Homo sapiens said. "Come here. I'm going to cut your hair."

"AAAAAAW!"

They ran off to get their spears.

3

APARTMENTS
3D & 4B

Reo and Juliet

In kindergarten he was a cuddly little doll who brought his lunch wrapped up like a present. Juliet remembered watching, entranced, as his small fingers untied the knot of the pretty patterned cloth. Inside was a shiny box. When he lifted the lid off, she'd gasped. Everything was tucked into tidy compartments — sandwich triangles, hard-boiled egg, three strawberries, a piece of roasted seaweed wrapped in cellophane.

Everything so perfect, like him!

Yet she didn't speak. She couldn't. And later, whenever she saw him in the hall of their apartment building, or in the playground, instead of saying hi, her whole head would turn into a big fat strawberry. They went to the same birthday parties, played in the same playground. Often they were in the same class. But she never spoke to him, only thought of him.

Reo Reo Reo Reo Reo ...

Year by year, the cuddly little doll grew. His legs elongated like an antelope's and the cuddliness became muscle. If they would have made a mismatched pair in kindergarten — bulky Juliet towering above doll-like Reo — by grade seven they were the same height, though Juliet was still bulkier.

But then she had to get braces, which gave her a new reason not to open her mouth. Her teeth were in jail, encased in wire, bound together with elastics.

Anyway, plenty of girls with straight teeth were interested in Reo by then. They lingered after school when the track-and-field team practiced. Sometimes two or three who didn't even live in their building would show up in the playground, hogging the swings, hoping he'd make an appearance on his balcony.

Juliet, who lived in 4B, saw them when she came out on her balcony, which was one floor above and to the left of 3D, where Reo lived. Though she could see onto his balcony, see the foldable patio table and chairs and the plants, Reo rarely showed himself.

Juliet would wave to the girls on the swings if she knew them. They'd wave back out of boredom, then leave.

•

Then they stopped coming, these other girls who were prettier and in love with Reo, too. Everybody stayed home.

One day Juliet was about to step outside when she noticed Reo on his balcony hunched on a patio chair, hood up, hands stuffed angrily in his pockets. She stayed where she was in her doorway, out of his sight, secretly watching. Admiring.

A few minutes later Reo's mom came out and said something in Japanese. She was only about as tall as Reo sitting down, but her angry expression would have scared Juliet if she were in his place.

He answered her in English. "But I'm supposed to be training!"

She talked some more while Reo ripped leaves off a plant and tossed them over the balcony. His mom scolded him for that, too. Then they both went inside.

Juliet felt his pain, which was how she knew she truly loved him. Because she hated sports, *especially* running — jiggling all over and gasping for air, the strawberry head and agonizing side stitches. She liked staying home. Her pops called the three of them homebodies.

But it had to be hard for Reo, an athlete.

That night at dinner, Juliet and her parents discussed how to get through the crisis. School was online now, restaurants and nonessential stores all closed. Many people were laid off or working from home. You could go out if you had to go to work, or to buy food or medicine, or walk a pet. Otherwise, everybody was supposed to stay inside.

"Let's do more than survive this," Juliet's mom said. "Let's use this time to achieve something."

"You're not talking about losing weight, are you?" Pops asked.

"No, this isn't the time for dieting. Too stressful!"

Juliet and Pops exchanged relieved glances. They were a jiggly family and okay with it.

"I mean, if there's something you've always wanted to do, now's the time." Mom gave both of them a sly smile.

"Is there something you've always wanted to do, Mom?"

"As a matter of fact, yes. I've always wanted to write a novel."

Juliet hadn't known this. Her mom had worked as an education coordinator at the YWCA before all the classes were canceled. She always had a library book on the go, but she had never mentioned wanting to write one.

"Believe me, I've tried to write, but I always give up out of lack of discipline. Or lack of courage." She stood up from the table. "No more. I'm starting my novel right now."

She strode out of the room, leaving Juliet and Pops to do the dishes.

Pops was a supply teacher, laid off, too. Juliet knew her parents worried about neither of them working and how long their savings would last. She'd heard them talking about it. Maybe writing was Mom's way of distracting herself. Or maybe she'd write a bestseller.

Juliet asked Pops, "Do you have something you've secretly wanted to do?"

"I'm pretty content, actually. I'll see if I can come up with something. What about you?"

"I wish I could be less shy," Juliet said.

Chuckling, Pops handed her another plate to dry. "You decide to become less shy while social distancing?"

"I could be less shy with *one* person," she said.

•

No, she couldn't. She peeked out and saw Reo on his balcony again, probably hiding from his parents. Her head started to swell and redden. Her caged teeth ached. She backed into the apartment.

But there was something familiar about the way he was leaning over the railing.

The previous summer her parents had taken her to see *Romeo and Juliet* at Shakespeare in the Park. They'd sat together on a picnic blanket on the grass in the middle of a modern city, but Juliet may as well have been in Renaissance Verona. Later, she asked if she'd been named for the Juliet in the play and was disappointed to hear that they'd just liked the name.

"Don't get any ideas," Pops said, meaning she shouldn't run off and marry a boy she'd only known for twenty-four hours, then drink poison because of him.

The most famous scene — even more famous than the poison drinking — was the balcony scene where

Romeo climbs over the garden wall and stands under Juliet's balcony and they pledge their love.

This Juliet had been waiting on her balcony for practically her whole life! What a *boring* play her life would make! And what would those not-shy girls hanging out on the swings have done in her place? At least they would have said something.

Juliet pictured her mom striding off to write. She threw back her shoulders and strode out on the balcony.

"Hi!"

Reo looked up, squinting at her. So handsome! Her head was already swelling, cheeks burning.

"I'm Juliet," she blurted.

He looked confused. "I know who you are."

"You do?"

"Of course."

"You've never talked to me before."

"You've never talked to me."

Good point. Juliet mentally groped around for something not-pathetic to say next. "How's it going?"

"Terrible," he said.

Juliet was doing great! This was possibly the best day of her whole life! She couldn't tell him that, of course.

Instead she asked, "What's wrong?"

"What's wrong? I'm in the Junior Development Program. And I'm thirteen, which is the optimal trainability window for my age group. I'm supposed to run the 5,000 meters at the track championships in June, which is less than two months away. I've got to run thirty miles a week to be ready for it. And my mom won't let me leave the apartment!"

He tore a leaf off a plant and threw it over the railing. "*That's* what's wrong."

"But we're supposed to stay in," Juliet said.

"You can go out if you have a good reason, which I do."

Reo's mom was right, Juliet thought, but she was desperate to say something encouraging. "Could you get a treadmill?"

"Duh," he said, not even bothering to meet her eye now. "Everything's closed."

Strawberries splattered her cheeks. "Right. I forgot. Well … nice talking to you."

She went back inside where she lay down on the sofa, breathing carefully in case she exploded with happiness.

She'd done it! She'd spoken to him!

•

Juliet's mom was going to write five hundred words a day. She already had a thousand of them.

She told them about it when they settled together on the sofa to watch a movie, their six feet propped up on the coffee table like three pairs of birds of different species along a telephone line. Black birds, striped birds, polka-dot birds. A big bowl of buttery popcorn sat in the middle lap, Juliet's. She wasn't supposed to eat popcorn because of her braces, but was given a pass on

Saturday nights, as long as she used the Waterpik before bed.

From the outside, life really hadn't changed much. But inside Juliet? She was a different species of girl.

"Five hundred words is two pages," Mom said. "See, I've broken it down into an achievable daily goal, which is what you two should do. The average novel is 350 pages. So I'll get to the end in 175 days. About six months."

"Are we going to be stuck inside for six months?" Juliet asked, thinking of Reo.

Reo Reo Reo Reo Reo ...

"I hope not," Mom said. "But by the time we get back to normal, I'll have made a good start. Whatever you two are planning for this time — you don't have to tell me what it is if you don't want to — goal-setting helps."

Pops asked what kind of book it was.

Mom took a big handful of popcorn. "A romance! They sell the best. Everybody needs love in their lives, right?"

"So it's our story?" he said.

Mom laughed and leaned over Juliet to kiss his cheek, squashing Juliet in the process.

Juliet didn't say she'd already achieved her goal.

But what about Reo, who had seen his goal crushed? How terrible!

•

The next day, when she noticed Reo slumped on the patio chair, she stepped out on her balcony with a calculator. "I've been thinking about you."

Arms crossed, scowling, he ignored her. Of course he did! Why would he talk to a girl whose face changed color every three sentences? Who had a hardware store in her mouth?

She almost retreated, but then she noticed the cord snaking from his hoodie pocket. It split and disappeared inside the hood.

She leaned right over the railing for a gargantuan two-armed wave. He saw her then and, looking annoyed, pulled his earbuds out.

"I've been thinking about you," she told him.

He stared blankly.

"You have an achievable goal. You just need to work toward it. I measured our balcony. It's ten feet long, so yours is too. If you run back and forth 264 times, you'll know how long it takes to run a mile. Then you can calculate how many hours you'd need to run to reach your goal of thirty miles per week."

"Run back and forth here?" His gesture took in the balcony around him. "For thirty miles?"

"Or you can run back and forth in the apartment, but your family probably wouldn't like it. Also, whoever lives below you might complain."

"Sounds really boring."

"What else do you have to do? I'll count. When should we start?" Juliet smiled with a closed mouth.

Reo sat in silence for a moment, thinking very handsomely.

Then he stood and began to fold the furniture and move the plants to clear the widest track possible.

He squinted up at her. "I have to change."

Juliet would cherish her whole life the first time that Reo ran for her. (Or so she thought at the time.) His dizzying shuttle back and forth, bare legs bulging, the hint of the cuddly doll he used to be when his cheeks filled up with air. The way his chest rose and fell, like hers as it swelled with love. She was free, free to adore him as she ticked off each lap on the pad.

Those other girls who hung around when the track team was practicing? They had to pretend they'd just happened to pass by. Juliet was practically his coach!

At one point, Pops reared up like a grizzly in the balcony doorway, but she waved away the distraction so she wouldn't lose count. If an actual grizzly had appeared, she would probably have done the same.

"Two-hundred and sixty-two," she called. "Two-hundred and sixty-three. Two-hundred and sixty-four. Stop!"

Reo was peeved when Juliet read out the time. "I can run a mile way faster than that. It's all that pivoting. Also, you can't really get your speed up."

She smiled, forgetting about the elastics and wires. Because it sounded like he was trying to impress her, or at least that he cared what she thought.

His conclusion: running for thirty miles a week at

ten-foot intervals was too humiliating. He went inside to stretch and shower.

"Don't give up so easily!" Juliet called.

When she went back in, Pops was at the table writing something on a pad of paper.

"Sorry," she told him. "I was busy. Did you want to talk to me?"

"Just going shopping. Anything you want to add to the list?"

Pops was their designated shopper. It was safer if only one person went to the grocery store. Then only one person in the family would risk exposure to the virus. Pops had not given Juliet and her mom any choice about this.

While Juliet read over the list, Pops got ready. He fitted a mask over his nose and mouth. He plucked a pair of medical gloves from the tissue-box receptacle and struggled to get them on his huge hands. Lastly, he donned a face shield that he'd made himself out of a clear plastic folder. It had three holes along one side so that it could be snapped into a three-ring binder. Through two of them he threaded the arms of his glasses.

"There," he said, words muffled by the mask. "Behold your knight in shining plastic and latex. Anything missing from the list?"

Juliet shook her head and handed it to him. He lumbered toward the door.

"Wait," she said.

Pops turned around. Juliet went and planted a kiss on his pillowy cheek through the shield, leaving a glistening imprint of her lip balm on the plastic.

"You're my hero," she told him.

•

The next morning Juliet easily talked Reo into running, though the fact that he came out on the balcony in his track clothes suggested he might have decided it for himself. *Any* amount of running was better than none. He would still be going to the track championships in better shape than most of the competition, except the ones who had big yards or lived in the country.

"But they probably don't have your discipline," Juliet said. "They're probably playing video games. My mom's writing a novel. She says discipline and courage are the most important things."

Reo nodded. "She's right."

Juliet beamed, remembering to cover her mouth with her hand. "How many hours a day do you want to run?"

"Two?"

She gave him the thumbs up.

"Let's get to it, then," he said, slapping his bare muscled thighs and standing. He folded up the chair he'd been sitting on. "Timer on?"

"Timer's on!"

It was like they were partners in a school project. Balcony running had been her idea, after all. She did her schoolwork while he ran and kept her other eye on the clock.

She called out encouragement. "Twenty minutes! Good work!"

"Almost an hour! You're doing great!"

"Only ten minutes to go! What a star!"

Afterward, he went inside to stretch and shower. He came back with an enormous pile of food, which he ate while listening to his music, his head bowed over the plate, the delicate doll replaced by a ravenous teenager who chewed with his mouth open.

If it had been anyone else, Juliet would have been too disgusted to watch, but she stayed, hoping that when he finished eating, they might talk.

What would they talk about? Juliet wanted to tell him that she was scared. Their building was across from the hospital. Though her and Reo's apartments were at the back of the building, they heard the ambulances arriving more and more often now, all day and into the night. Pops listened to news updates on the radio, keeping the volume low if she was in the room. To protect her, Juliet knew.

Reo must be scared, too.

He wiped his mouth on the back of his hand, got up from the table and carried the empty plate inside.

"See you tomorrow!" Juliet called.

•

Only a few days later her dream came true, the one she'd dreamed that night at Shakespeare in the Park. She heard her name called from beneath her balcony.

"Juliet!"

She let her spoon fall in her bowl and rushed out, careful to keep one hand over her mouth because there would be gross granola bits stuck all over her braces.

"Reo?" She leaned right over the railing toward where he stood, below and across.

"I'm getting out!"

"You mean *outside*?"

"Yes! You know that kid Louis on the first floor? He's renting out his dog."

"And your mom's letting you?"

"I have to wear a mask, which sucks, because it will affect my time. But whatever, right?"

Juliet felt Reo's joy just as she had felt his pain. "That's so wonderful! Can I come?"

"What do you mean? Run with me?" He let out a sharp laugh, like he'd never heard anything so ridiculous.

She didn't know *what* she meant. She'd just blurted it out, because they were partners. "I can wait in the lobby. I'll time you."

"No, that's okay," Reo said, and he went back inside.

Juliet stood there for a moment, no longer swept up in Reo's joy, and hers for him. She actually didn't want to leave the safety of the apartment. She was afraid to and, anyway, Pops would never let her.

But the way Reo had fired his no at her felt like a stinging elastic.

It stung the whole day.

That night Mom came into Juliet's room with a sheaf of paper in her hand and her reading glasses perched on her head. They held back her hair, which needed cutting.

"Could I get some feedback, honey?"

Mom had finished the first chapter of her novel. "I read it to Pops. He says I'll be getting the Nobel Prize next year. Sweet, but not very helpful. Can I read it to you?"

Juliet closed her own book, which she was having trouble concentrating on anyway. She sat up on the bed to make room for Mom. The two of them settled side by side with their backs against the wall, causing the mattress to roil so that they fell into each other, giggling.

Juliet started to feel better.

Mom lowered her glasses and began to read. "'*All True Dreams*.' That's just the working title.

"'Sara glanced at her reflection in the rearview mirror. Did she look okay for her date with Steve? Every blond hair was in place. Her lipstick stayed within the lines. But that furtive glance changed everything. The car in front, a brand-new BMW, stopped suddenly and Sara's old clunker ran right into it!'"

Juliet began to slide down the wall. Mom read on, not noticing.

What was Juliet supposed to say? It got worse and worse until the chapter ended with the two characters exchanging insurance information and phone numbers, Sara's heart racing with excitement.

"Isn't that a great setup?" Mom asked.

"She's not going to call him, is she?" Juliet said.

"Why not?"

"He yelled at her. She didn't dent his car on purpose."

Mom wasn't offended. "That's the character arc, honey. Leonardo starts out a jerk, but by the end he's a changed man."

"But why's her heart racing with excitement over a jerk?"

"Good point. I thought it would be less creepy if she made the first move. I guess I have to figure out a better reason for Sara to call. Maybe there's a problem with her insurance? Maybe it's lapsed?"

Mom flipped the pages over and asked Juliet to pass her the pencil lying on the side table. She jotted some notes.

"Can she have brown hair?" Juliet asked.

"Sure. Good suggestion. Keep talking. I'm writing everything down. This is so helpful, honey."

After she noted a few more of Juliet's suggestions, Mom said, "Romances are supposed to be a bit corny and contrived. They're not really about love. Love is a completely different thing. Remember when we went to see *Romeo and Juliet*? Those two didn't even *know* each other."

When Mom mentioned the play, Juliet thought not of Reo, but Pops. Pops the last time he went out for groceries, valiantly suiting up in his protective gear. After he left the apartment, Juliet realized they were out of popcorn and hurried out to the balcony.

"Pops!" she called down just as he came trudging out the back of the building.

He stopped, looked around, then up. When he saw her, he placed a gloved hand over his heart and pretended to stagger.

"Dost I hear fair Juliet?" he shouted.

•

After her conversation with Mom, Juliet searched the play online and discovered it was actually Juliet who had called out to Romeo.

"O Romeo, Romeo, wherefore art thou Romeo?"

Anyway, Reo was no Romeo. He was just her neighbor.

The next day the school board sent an email. With great regret, they informed parents and students that all upcoming school activities and events had to be canceled. First on the list were elementary and high-school graduation ceremonies. Juliet felt a spasm of disappointment.

Music festivals
Science fairs
Field trips
Track-and-field meets

Later, she heard the sound of somebody crying. She thought it was coming from the playground, until she remembered that the playground was taped off.

She stepped outside.

"Juliet!"

Reo wiped his face on his hoodie sleeve and stood up from his chair. "Did you get the email? They canceled the championships."

"Yeah. I read that."

He came over to the railing, craning to see her better. She stepped back inside.

"Everything's falling apart. It sucks so bad. But maybe I'll stick to my running goal anyway."

"You should," Juliet said from the doorway. "I'm helping my mom with her novel. A goal takes your mind off things."

"I mean I'll run here. On the balcony."

There was a long silence, soon filled with an ambulance siren.

After it stopped, Reo pushed his long hair out of his eyes to see her better. "It really helps my motivation having you here."

Juliet squirmed. "It's kind of boring."

He squinted up at her, handsome as ever, but still …

"I wondered about that," he said quietly.

She waited to hear what else he had to say.

"I get it. It's no fun watching other people do stuff, right?" Now he seemed embarrassed. He looked away. "It's just that I can't really talk when I run. It affects my time. And talking's hard for me anyway. But maybe sometime we can? Just talk-talk?"

Below in the playground, a bird landed on the monkey bars and began to sing.

"Okay," Juliet said. "When?"

"How about now?"

She stepped out on her balcony again. Reo settled back down on his chair.

"Are you scared, too?" he asked.

4

APARTMENT
3C

I Like Your Tie

When Conner found out they didn't have to go back to school after spring break, he couldn't stop fist pumping. Instead of math and socials and, worst of all, language (f)arts, instead of Mr. Faizabadi with his weirdo ties coming over and tapping his finger on Conner's desk, Conner was going to surf the couch right into summer watching the hockey playoffs.

Keep it coming, Virus! Maybe Faizabadi would get canned. That would be the icing on the doughnut.

Instead, Conner's dad got canned when all the restaurants closed.

There was a good side to this, though. His dad used to work really long hours. Conner and his little sister Eden barely saw him except on Sundays and Mondays, his days off. Now Conner and his dad could couch surf the playoffs *together*. Way to go, Virus! Life was getting better and better.

But then the worst thing Conner could think of happened. Actually, he wouldn't in a zillion years have thought of this. It was *inconceivable*, according to that thesaurus exercise in language (f)arts.

Hockey playoffs were canceled.

•

On what was supposed to be the first day back at school, Mr. Faizabadi emailed all the kids with worksheets and links to homework sites. *Drop me a line anytime you need to*, he wrote. *And hang in there! Zoom classes will be starting in a few weeks.*

Not canned, obviously.

While Conner was reading the email, Dad shuffled into the kitchen in his robe, feeling around in his pocket for his cigarettes with one hand, rubbing his stubbly head with the other. He still wasn't out of the habit of sleeping late. Also, Mom said he was depressed about getting laid off. Conner, too, because of hockey. Thanks for nothing, Virus!

Dad headed for the balcony to smoke.

"You're not playing a video game, are you?" he said in passing.

"What if I am?" Conner answered.

Dad stopped and pointed a finger right at Conner. "No."

"No what?" Conner said. "I just asked you a question. You asked *me* one, didn't you?"

"No *attitude*, Loudboy." Loudboy was what Dad called Conner when he was mad at him. "And no sitting in front of the computer all day long."

"It's homework, dude," Conner said under his breath.

With a sigh and a shake of his stubble, Dad went outside.

He was in a better mood when he returned. Conner should have known not to say anything to him before that first smoke.

"Okay," Dad said. "Here's what's happening. You guys are going to school. Here." He meant the kitchen table cluttered with breakfast dishes and cereal boxes. Nobody had put the milk back in the fridge. "I'm going to be the teacher. Eden!"

She came running. He told her what was happening, ordered them to clean up and get their school work together, then poured himself a coffee and went to dress.

They decided to start with math. "Get the worst thing over with, right?" Dad said.

Conner printed out Eden's worksheets and she attacked them. He looked at his own on the screen. It took about ten seconds for him to push the laptop away and cross his arms over his chest.

"You barely looked at it," Dad said.

Dad pulled the computer across the table. They were word problems, which were the hardest because you had to be a good reader as well as good at math. Dad's eyebrows sank as he read. When you don't have hair, just stubble from shaving off what hair is left, your eyebrows are more obvious.

Those eyebrows made it obvious that Dad didn't understand the questions either.

He closed the laptop. "You know what always helped me back when I had to suffer through this? Doing real stuff. Stuff that has a point. Not a bunch of abstract questions about people driving from A to B, or buying apples in the store."

"Can we go to the grocery store with you?" Eden asked.

"No. It's not safe. And you're in school at the moment, remember? I'm trying to teach you some *useful* math. Eden, get a roll of toilet paper from the cupboard. Conner, find an empty box."

Now Conner was curious. He had a bunch of shoeboxes in the room he shared with Eden, for storing hockey cards and other stuff. He emptied one out and brought it back to the kitchen.

"Perfect," Dad said.

Eden came back with the package of toilet paper. Three rolls left.

Dad's useful math activity? Take a roll of toilet paper, tear off two squares, put them in the box, and keep doing it until all the toilet paper is piled in the shoebox. They were supposed to count how many double squares went into the box.

Halfway through this *inconceivably* dumb exercise, Conner quit.

Dad's eyebrows lowered again, this time with disapproval.

Conner pointed to the package sitting on the table. "It says right there. Two hundred and forty-two sheets per roll. You just have to divide it by two."

"I can't divide hundreds," Eden said.

"Break it down," Conner told her. He flipped her worksheet over and wrote: 242 = 200+40+2. "If that's too scary, you can even go smaller."

He wrote: 100+100+20+20+1+1.

Eden's eyes grew big. It was like a magic trick to her, especially when Conner told her it would be even easier if she made the last zero disappear when she was adding and made it reappear at the end.

"Is that allowed?" she said.

"Yeah. Mr. Faizabadi showed us." Faizabadi was actually a pretty good math teacher. Conner gave him that.

Dad interrupted. "Do you want to teach this class, Conner? Because if you do, go ahead."

He stood up from the table and stalked back out onto the balcony for another smoke.

•

At the end of the day, when Mom came home from work, Eden went running to her. "Daddy's our substitute teacher! We're doing school at the kitchen table!"

Mom looked so happy until Eden said, "And Conner got in trouble just like at real school!"

Conner was lying on the sofa watching skateboard videos on the laptop. He pretended not to see Mom's disappearing smile. If Conner hadn't chased it away, the fact that Dad hadn't cooked dinner would have.

Dad was in their bedroom. Mom knocked and opened the door. "I thought you were going to cook now that you're home."

From inside, Dad said, "I was teaching the kids."

Conner snorted.

A few minutes later Mom came back, out of her UPS uniform now, and started making dinner herself. She called Conner over.

"I'm going to show you how to use the rice maker. Things are really busy at work and we could use the overtime pay."

"Why can't Dad do it?" Conner asked. "He's only teaching us for about an hour."

She turned to him and stroked his cheek with the back of her hand. She used to kiss the top his head, but he was as tall as her now even though he was only in grade five.

"I need you to help out and not get on Dad's nerves. This could be a special time for you two. Okay?"

Conner nodded. He'd try. He really would.

•

The next day Conner realized there was another reason for Dad's toilet-paper exercise. They were running out.

There wasn't any toilet paper at the store either. Dad had gone into three stores and none of them had TP.

He said it was called hoarding and that it was stupid because there actually was plenty of toilet paper to go around.

"I mean, before this virus thing? Did you ever go into a drugstore or supermarket that had no toilet paper?"

After they finished putting away the groceries, he picked up the shoebox with the toilet paper.

"This is called rationing. They used to ration everything during the war."

"What war?" Conner asked.

"Can you speak to me in a respectful tone for a change?" Dad snapped.

Conner winced. He was just asking a simple question! There had been a lot of wars!

"We're only going to use two squares of toilet paper at a time," Dad told Eden.

"But what about number two?" Eden wailed. "Two squares aren't enough!"

"Obviously if two don't do the job, you can use more. Rationing is to stop you and your mom from using half the roll every time you pee."

Conner smirked. Quickly, he straightened his face before Dad noticed.

Except Dad did see the smirk. This time, instead of snapping, he smirked back. Rationing was for the girls. So Conner and Dad were a team again, with regards to toilet paper, anyway.

Conner felt good about that — as good as when Mom stroked his cheek. Maybe life wasn't so different after all.

If they did run out of toilet paper, though, life would be *inconceivable*.

Dad clapped his hands together. "Time for school. I'm just going for a smoke first."

He'd only been out on the balcony a couple of minutes when Conner heard him calling.

"Look," Dad said, as Conner stepped out. Smoke spurted from his nostrils, dragon-like. What happened to his good mood?

Two ambulances were parked in front of the hospital across the street, one with the back door open. They must have just brought somebody in.

Not for the first time, Conner wished they lived on the other side of the building. He felt bad whenever he saw a stretcher lifted out of the ambulance. He didn't know what to do with the feeling. Usually he went inside and found Eden and sat on her because it was easier to deal with a screaming seven-and-a-half-year-old than to see somebody who might be dying. Who might already be dead.

But Dad wasn't talking about the hospital. He pointed to the street below. Conner leaned over the railing and saw the white top of somebody's head.

It was Mrs. Watts, who lived on the first floor and gave out the most candy at Hallowe'en. She was fishing in her purse for her keys, a wheeled shopping cart beside her.

Sticking out the top of it was a 12-roll package of toilet paper.

"Do the math on that TP," Dad said.

"For the whole package?" Conner said. "I'd need a calculator."

"Eyeballing it, I'd say she — one little old lady who lives all by herself — is hoarding toilet paper at the expense of a family of four. I saw her a couple of days ago with toilet paper, too."

"If we run out," Conner joked, "I know whose door to knock on."

"Don't," Dad said. "Don't have anything to do with *people like that*. Go tell your sister school's starting."

Conner left his father staring down at Mrs. Watts, an ugly lemon-sucking expression on his face.

•

In Mr. Faizabadi's next email he recommended that they all watch *Cloudy with a Chance of Meatballs* on Netflix starting at 1:00. Then it would be like their Last Friday of the Month Movie Club.

Conner was missing school by then and would have watched, except Dad took the laptop into the bedroom and closed the door. He said he was educating himself on all this "crap" that was coming down.

Conner was even starting to miss Mr. Faizibadi! Up until the virus, which was officially ruining his life now, he'd thought being a teacher was a wussy kind of job. All you had to do was stand in front of a bunch of kids and tell them stuff you'd learned yourself way back when. If they didn't listen, you were twice as big. You could just sit on them or something, like Conner did with Eden. How hard could that be?

But now Conner knew there were actual skills involved.

One was dressing like a teacher.

Mr. Faizabadi always wore a shirt and tie. Conner had made a lot of sarcastic comments about his ties even though some of them were pretty cool, like the soccer ball tie and the one with the solar system. One had a twisty ladder on it that Mr. Faizabadi explained was the double-helix of DNA. DNA was the genes you inherit from your parents that made you who you were.

Unlike Mr. Faizabadi, Dad wore sweatpants and a T-shirt when he taught them. The same sweatpants and T-shirt every day.

At first Conner was even worse. He didn't get out of his pajamas the whole day! But then he looked on the school-board website for tips to help Dad with his substitute teaching and read this: *Disruptions in routines can be stressful. Keeping to a schedule helps maintain a sense of normalcy and stability. Get your children dressed and ready for school even though they're at home.*

So Conner started dressing every morning. He brushed his teeth, too. He might have been the only person in the family doing this, other than Mom. As he brushed, he tried to imagine which crazy tie Mr. Faizabadi had on that day. The DNA tie? A few times he thought about emailing and asking him to send out a picture every morning to help with class morale, but Mr. Faizabadi would probably think he was being sarcastic.

Another teacher skill was patience. Mr. Faizabadi had learned that on the job. At the beginning of the year, he used to send Conner to the office. One day he lost his temper and yelled.

Later, he apologized, which was weird.

"I think I'm starting to get you, Conner," he said.

After that, whenever Conner was "disruptive," or about to be, Mr. Faizabadi would saunter past and tap Conner's desk. For some reason, it always shut him up.

Dad had about as much patience as he had hair. After the incident with Mrs. Watts, he got frustrated helping Eden with fractions. Instead of trying to explain them a different way, he just explained louder. Conner rolled his eyes, which was when Mr. Faizabadi would have expertly deployed the Tap.

Dad said, "What's your problem?"

Conner pointed at his own homework on the screen. "These problems are my problem, dude."

"Yeah? Well, try this one then, Loudboy."

Dad grabbed the saltshaker, unscrewed the lid and poured out a pile in the middle of the table. "I want you to count every grain and keep your mouth shut while you do it."

"Counting isn't math for somebody in grade five," Conner said, to which Dad replied, "How would you like me to pour all that salt down your throat?"

"Daddy, don't!" Eden said.

Conner put his head down and pretended to count. His hands shook, which made separating the grains harder.

•

The day after the salt incident, they didn't have kitchen-table school. Conner got dressed and brushed his teeth for nothing.

Dad wasn't like this before — mad all the time. Mostly he was a nice guy. Conner knew he was acting like this because he'd lost his job, because, like the school-board website said, *Disruptions in routines can be stressful.* And no hockey!

When there was no *normalcy and stability*, sometimes it affected a person's mental health. Conner said jerky things too when he felt stressed, which happened whenever he didn't understand something they were doing in class. It was like somebody else's tongue took over his mouth. He felt smart as he was saying the jerky thing, but not when he saw the other person's face.

This might have been in his DNA because Dad had the same problem. And not just with Conner.

The grocery stores decided that old people should be allowed to shop before everybody else because they were more likely to die of the virus. This meant that Mrs. Watts got first crack at the toilet paper at a time when everybody in Conner's house was starting to worry about wiping with store flyers or leaves off the houseplants.

Dad was having his first smoke of the day out on the balcony when Mrs. Watts came home from shopping. There probably wasn't even any toilet paper in her cart. It looked pretty empty.

Still, the sight of her pulling her cart along set Dad off. He started pelting her with insults.

Thankfully, it was Mom's day off because it took both her and Conner to drag Dad back inside. He stormed out of the apartment, though everybody was supposed to stay home. So no school that day either.

After Dad left, Conner couldn't stop thinking about Mrs. Watts. He kept picturing her shocked face looking up at them, white and wrinkly like one those crepe paper flowers Conner made in art.

They worried all day about Dad. Mom tried calling his cell phone. It rang in the bedroom.

Around suppertime, he finally showed up. Though he didn't apologize, he brought pizza, which was sort of the same thing. Mom convinced him that he would feel better if he had a shower and changed his clothes before they ate, which was when Conner slipped out.

He went downstairs and knocked on Mrs. Watts's door. Her apartment faced the playground, wrapped in yellow tape now. In the summer she always sat on her little patio with her flowers and watched the kids play. She wasn't officially babysitting. Nobody paid her. But some of the parents in the building let their kids play on their own because they knew Mrs. Watts was close by.

Standing at her door, Conner felt even more terrible than when he saw her shocked paper-flower face.

He felt ashamed, for Dad and for himself.

Finally, he knocked and, after a minute, he heard steps. Then the scrape of the peephole cover.

"Mrs. Watts? It's Conner from the third floor," he began. "I want to apologize for those things my dad said to you this morning. We are in a stressful situation like lots of people. He didn't mean it. I'm really sorry."

He waited for her to say something back, but she didn't, so he pressed on with the other thing.

"Mrs. Watts? One of the stressful things is that we only have thirty-four squares of toilet paper left. I know because we're counting. If you have any extra, could I buy it off you? I have twenty dollars with me and a lot of change."

A long pause. The peephole scraped closed.

Why would she sell him her toilet paper? Dad had yelled horrible things at her loud enough for the whole neighborhood to hear. Conner didn't blame her one bit.

He was already walking away when he heard the chain rattle. Mrs. Watts's door opened and a jumbo package of toilet paper slid through the gap. The door closed again.

He ran over, babbling, "Thank you, thank you, thank you! How much —"

"No charge," he heard.

When he got back to the apartment, he didn't say anything about scoring the TP. He was afraid it would set Dad off again. He just left a roll on the back of the toilet and put the rest in the cupboard.

They had a pretty normal supper after that. "Before normal." Not "now normal."

It scared Conner to think that the "now normal" might become just "normal."

While they ate, they talked about how lucky they were. Mom was still working. They had an affordable place to live even though it was a bit cramped. They were healthy and if anything did happen, there was a good hospital right across the street.

After dinner, Mom suggested playing UNO, which kept Dad away from the news. The rising number of cases stressed him out even more. So did the wails of the ambulances on the news reports mixing with the real ambulances outside.

If there had been hockey, they could have watched that instead.

•

Conner was waking up early now. He didn't use to. Before, Mom had to call a tow truck to drag him out of bed. But now that he didn't have a place to get to on time, his eyes popped open.

Everybody else was still asleep, including Eden in the bunk below him.

He just lay there thinking, *Wow! Nothing bad has happened yet.* Or if it had, he didn't know about it yet, so he stayed in bed for as long as he could.

Apart from the ambulances, the city was quiet now that everybody was staying home. There were hardly any cars, even downtown. The main morning noise was birds. It would be totally silent. Then one of them started belting it out. Conner guessed that first one was like an army bugler. Suddenly, they were all singing away, *la la la*, not giving a cheep for all the messed-up humans.

That morning, the day after Dad took off, it seemed like the happiest sound in the world.

Mom was first up. She showered and dressed in her uniform. When Conner came out to say goodbye, she told him to call her if he was worried about anything.

"I wish I didn't have to go to work, Conner. But all this overtime will really help until normal returns."

Would it return?

Eden woke up next. Conner tried to make her get dressed, but no way. Then he tried to get her to the table for school.

"You're not my teacher! Dad is!"

"I'm substituting for the substitute today," he said.

Conner tried sitting on her, but she started screaming and he was afraid she'd wake Dad. He left her playing with her dolls and went and put an ear to Dad's door. He was already awake. Conner could hear him tapping the computer keys and muttering to himself.

It was nearly an hour before Dad came out of his room with his laptop under his arm. He set it on the kitchen table and poured himself some coffee.

Conner asked, "Are we having school today?"

Dad said, "Isn't it Saturday?"

"Is it?" Conner said.

"See?" said Eden, who was eating her cereal. "It's Saturday. I don't have to go to school."

After Dad went out on the balcony for his smoke, Conner opened the laptop to see if Mr. Faizabadi had sent new work.

He saw then that it was Monday.

The page that came up on Dad's computer was a chat room called VIRUS HOAX. Conner couldn't help reading some of the comments.

Freedomluver: Its all FAKE NEWS!!!

Mike237: Not. Its made in China, just like everything we buy.

GlennBware: You got it Mike. And the Terrorists bought it. They couldn't bring us to our knees with planes. Now they got us —

That was as far as Conner read of Dad's post when he heard the balcony door open. He shut the computer and pretended to be reading Eden's worksheet. The numbers swirled in front of his eyes. He felt like throwing up.

Did Mom know about this? He had to think of an excuse to phone her.

"We need more printer paper," Conner said after his father refilled his coffee mug and came to get the laptop. "Can I call Mom and ask her to pick some up?"

Dad drew his cell phone from his bathrobe pocket. "Just leave it on the counter when you're done. Don't bother me. I'm doing something."

He disappeared into the bedroom.

Conner took the phone out on the balcony so Eden wouldn't hear him.

"Again?" Mom said. "I told him to stop reading that stuff. It's poisonous. It's *dangerous*. Ask him to teach you again."

"He says it's Saturday."

She sighed. "Hang in there. Don't wind him up the way you do. I'll be back by six-thirty or seven. I've already told them I have to stay home tomorrow."

That left Conner with six hours to try to keep his mouth shut.

Nothing went wrong until the end of the day, except that Dad smoked about twice as many cigarettes as he usually did and while he smoked, he leaned over the balcony railing and stared at the back of the hospital, muttering. Every time an ambulance came, he swore.

By six o'clock Conner was listening so hard for Mom to come home, he thought his ears would start bleeding.

At seven o'clock every morning and seven o'clock at night the shift changed at the hospital. A bunch of doctors and nurses and paramedics and cleaners all left the building, keeping a safe distance apart. The new bunch entered.

It turned out Conner wasn't the only one with his

eye on the clock because at ten to seven, when quite a few of the incoming workers had gathered and were waiting outside, Dad went back out on the balcony. His pack of smokes was still lying on the table.

Did Conner know what was going to happen? He must have sensed it, because what came to mind when Dad slipped outside was something that had happened months ago at school.

Mr. Faizabadi walked into the classroom wearing his cool molecule tie, smiling and greeting everybody.

Nobody said hi back. They either had a weird embarrassed expression on their faces, or they were staring at their desks.

Conner snickered behind his hand.

So Mr. Faizabadi glanced over his shoulder and saw was written on the board. Slowly, he turned. There were just five untrue words written there, but for a full minute maybe (it felt like an hour), he stood with his back to them.

Some kids squirmed. Some held their breath. Conner did, too.

But nothing happened, so Conner began to wonder why he'd done it.

Finally, Mr. Faizabadi picked up the eraser and erased the words.

Then he said, "Who's up for some math?"

The weird thing was that Dad started yelling *almost the same thing*. That the hospital workers waiting to start their shift were all a bunch of terrorists. That they were the ones making everybody sick. Somehow it had gotten twisted up in his mind.

Conner tried to pull him back inside, but he wasn't strong enough. The only thing he could do was drown Dad out so that the workers waiting across the street wouldn't hear him yelling.

Already one or two were looking up at the building, wondering what was going on.

Conner ran inside and grabbed what he could find that would make a lot of noise. He ran back out and started banging a ladle against a pot lid.

"THANK YOU!" he yelled. "THANK YOU!"

Eden joined them on the balcony.

"Thank you!" she screamed. She *loved* to scream. Then she tore back inside for something to bang.

The most amazing thing happened then. The big double doors opened and the workers who had just finished their shift began to leave. They looked up at where the clanging and banging and shouting was coming from — Conner's balcony — and they smiled and waved along with the workers waiting to go in.

At the same time, Claudia and her little brother in the next apartment stepped out on their balcony with pot lids. On the balcony below, Jessica and her family came out to make noise, too. Soon everybody who lived at the front of the building had joined in.

It was just like with the birds — one starts it off, and in a few minutes the whole sky explodes in sound. People in the apartment building next door began coming out, everybody calling, "THANK YOU! THANK YOU! THANK YOU!"

Dad had already stopped yelling. He seemed stunned and a little ashamed and really, really tired. He leaned against the wall and closed his eyes. Conner stopped banging his pot lid. Dad was crying.

"Daddy, what's the matter?" Eden asked.

He hugged both of them so tight Conner could hardly breathe.

"Kids?" he said. "I think I need some help."

•

To: m.faizabadi@sd25.ca
From: loudboy2009@gmail.com
Dear Mr. F,
I guess you cant tell who this is. Or maybe you can hahah!!!! Conner. I just wanted to say I'm stoaked about zoomin tomorrow. We already downloaded the app. My dad zooms with his countsiler. that's why we got it. I cant wait to see your tie!

An 1 more thing. I forgot to say it a long time ago. Sorry.

You know Y I thinl.

ps Im been serious. I promise

5

APARTMENT
1C

The Entrepreneur's Bible

Not everybody was unhappy about staying home. Some of the building's residents — mainly the ones with fur, feathers or scales, who had previously spent most of the day alone — loved it.

In Apartment 4A, Gingersnap was thrilled that the humans were around. Now he could drape himself over the keyboard when somebody was using the computer, or a book when somebody was trying to read. Or he could curl up on somebody's lap just as they showed signs of wanting to get up off the sofa.

Now that everybody stayed home, Gingersnap purred all day long.

The quiet woman in 4C had a budgie named Namaste. The family next door (Gingersnap's) could sometimes hear Namaste reciting poetry in his cage while the quiet woman (they never heard *her*) was at work: "I wandered lonely as a cloud! Lonely as a cloud!" But now that the quiet woman worked from home, Namaste had learned to say, "Six feet back, please. Six feet back!" He was also learning "Happy Birthday," which took the same length of time to sing twice as it took to wash the virus off your hands.

Sweet Pea, the only dog in the building, lived in 1C. Of a miscellaneous breed — mop-like dark brown fur, stubby legs and a pushed-in face — she was sweet like her name, friendly with everybody no matter their species.

She was also shaped like her name because, with Louis in school and his mom at her salon, she was rarely walked. Of course she was taken out to go to the bathroom and check her pee-mail, then to the playground behind the building where she would waddle around mooching pats and snacks from the kids. Goldfish crackers and cheese string were major contributors to her pea shape.

But that was before, when Sweet Pea used to spend most of the day alone at the apartment window, sighing. Now that Louis and his mom, Angelique, were staying home, Sweet Pea was ecstatic.

Sadly, Sweet Pea's ecstasy was Louis' mom's misery. Angelique was sick with worry. What if Louis caught the virus? What if she did? They lived right across from the hospital where the really sick people ended up.

And what if her salon had to permanently close? It had only been open for six months before the virus hit.

For most of Louis' life, his mom had worked for

other people, always saving money in the hope of becoming her own boss one day.

Finally her dream came true, thanks in part to Louis who, back when he was nine, had found a book in the free bin at the library called *The Entrepreneur's Bible*. Even though it wasn't a kids' book, he'd read it from cover to cover (395 pages), often during church (they chose a back pew so nobody would notice). Now he knew more than most eleven-year-olds about starting and running a small business.

To start a small business you have to *take risks*. You should *expect to lose money* at first, until you establish yourself, which you will if you *find your niche* and *never stop networking*. If you are *flexible* and *confident* and *pay attention to market needs*.

There was nothing in *The Entrepreneur's Bible* about what to do if a pandemic hits before you *find your niche*. Nothing about *networking* when you have to stay six feet apart from everybody else. Nothing about how to *pay attention to market needs* when social distancing has shut the market down.

Louis checked the index: no pandemic! He could only be *flexible* and *confident*.

He looked online and found out which small business emergency support programs his mom qualified for. He downloaded the forms and helped her fill them out.

With the government money, Louis figured they would have enough for the next two months' rent. By then the virus would be gone and everything would go back to normal.

Right?

•

They were used to the sound of ambulances. Sirens were a background noise they rarely noticed.

Then they did notice. Because there were suddenly so many.

Louis walked with Sweet Pea to the mailbox on the corner to mail the government forms. They stopped to watch the paramedics in hazmat suits and face shields unloading stretchers from the line of arriving ambulances.

Sweet Pea sniffed the air and looked up at Louis as if to say, "What's going on?"

Louis felt afraid for the first time. He hurried on to the mailbox, practically dragging Sweet Pea, who couldn't run that fast. No way was he *not* going to mail those forms. Then he picked up Sweet Pea and jogged home with her in his arms.

That morning, Louis had lifted Sweet Pea up and set her on his mom's bed (the dog was too short and fat to jump up on her own). Sweet Pea woke Angelique with kisses. But Angelique just rolled over and pulled the pillow over her head, too worried and depressed to get out of bed.

She was up now, though still in her pajamas, clasping a mug of coffee in her hands, but forgetting to drink it. Sweet Pea wagged over to greet her, but Angelique was listening to the radio with wide eyes.

Louis sat on the sofa beside her.

"They passed more emergency measures," she told him.

Until then, they weren't supposed to gather with people they didn't already live with. They had to stay a strict six feet apart from everybody else. Face masks were recommended.

Now there was a new regulation: a total lockdown for the next three weeks. They weren't supposed to leave their homes at all, except to buy food or medicine, go to an essential workplace, or walk a pet.

Anybody caught outside the home for nonessential reasons would be fined.

"More money we don't have!" Angelique started to cry.

Louis pried the mug out of her hands before her coffee spilled.

"Maman," he said, smiling. "We're not going to get fined. We're obeying the rules."

Sweet Pea, at their feet, gave a reassuring yip.

Louis remembered then that they'd hurried to the mailbox so fast that Sweet Pea hadn't had the chance to do her business or check her pee-mail. They'd have to go out again. They had *to*.

More importantly, they *could*.

"Maman, look." He lifted Sweet Pea up. "We're *lucky*. We have a dog."

How many stories had he read in *The Entrepreneur's Bible* where the millionaire claimed, "Sure, I worked hard. But I was also *lucky*."?

Angelique got dressed and they took Sweet Pea out the back door of the building.

The sun was shining, the trees bursting into leaf. They kept walking until the sirens grew faint. The city seemed quiet then, not the cacophonous place it usually was.

Angelique put her arm around Louis' shoulder.

"You're right. We're so lucky to have Sweet Pea. A walk in the fresh air makes a person feel so much more positive."

"This is good, Maman. You're getting your confidence back. That's what every entrepreneur needs most."

"Don't they need money most?"

"Nope. Confidence. But money helps."

Sweet Pea pooped, and when Louis bent with the purple bag to pick it up, the idea came to him.

•

Feeling cooped up?
Want to keep physically fit and improve your mental health?
You need a walk in the fresh air!
So why not RENT A DOG today?
Our dog is sweet and friendly and fun to walk.
She does not bite!
Contact us to schedule your walk today!

Be flexible to market needs! Never stop networking!

Louis would stick with their building where he already had a network. He knew most of the other tenants at least by sight. The kids he knew by name. They all used to hang around together in the playground before the yellow tape went up.

He slipped a flyer under every door, then went back inside the apartment to wait for the phone to ring.

It took a few days before people understood the new regulation and before they did start to feel cooped up. Louis used that time to turn a scribbler into an appointment book and to research pricing.

The only service he could compare his to were ones where you paid to have your own dog walked, not the other way around. The going rate seemed to be $12 to $20 for a 30-minute walk.

"Maman!" Louis called. "It says here that a professional dog walker can make up to $80,000 a year!"

"No way!" Angelique said. "What am I doing cutting hair?"

Then a feature ran on the evening news about several joggers who had been fined. The phone rang.

Louis and Sweet Pea met their first customer in the lobby while maintaining a distance of six feet. Conner from 3C, his little sister and his dad. This was the family that started the building — the whole neighborhood, in fact — banging pots at 7:00 p.m. to thank the hospital workers for saving lives.

"Hi, Conner," Louis said.

"Hi, Louis."

"You know Sweet Pea."

"Sweet Pea!" Conner's little sister, Eden, crouched down and opened her arms. Louis dropped the leash so that Sweet Pea could waddle over and kiss her.

"I have to ask you to pay up front," Louis told Conner's dad.

"It's like the cop shows, Dad," Conner said. "The crooks get paid *before* they turn over the goods."

"Hey!" Louis said. "This is a legit business."

They all laughed. Conner's dad actually did look like a criminal — big and bulky with a shaved head. At least, it used to be shaved. Now sandy hair was growing in around the sides.

Conner's hair was growing, too, his eyes hidden behind his brown bangs. Same with Eden, who was sitting on the floor with Sweet Pea, rubbing the dog's round furry belly.

Before he accepted the money, Louis reminded Conner's dad about his special deal. "It's twenty bucks for thirty minutes, but only thirty bucks for an hour. The special start-up price."

Conner and his dad exchanged a look. His dad said, "Just a sec."

Father and son walked a few feet away and, turning their backs on Louis, conferred in low tones. Louis could hear some of it. Something about a counselor and needing exercise and could they afford it?

"What if we come back early?" Conner called to Louis.

"If you come back within the thirty minutes, you get a full refund for the extra ten. Five-minute grace period. Just call and let me know." He patted the phone in his pocket.

Conner's dad pulled another ten-dollar bill out of his front pocket. Louis held out the envelope he'd brought to safely collect the fees.

"Come on, Sweet Pea!" sang Eden, leading the dog away.

Sweet Pea looked back at Louis to check that it was okay. Just as Louis waved, the phone rang again.

Another booking already! He was sorry now that he'd pushed the hour-long deal, but *entrepreneurship is about learning on the go*.

He went back inside the apartment. It must have been Sunday, because Angelique was at Zoom church when he got in. When she looked inside the envelope, it was like she'd seen a miracle.

That night, after gobbling her food and drinking two bowls of water, Sweet Pea flopped down in her dog bed where she almost never slept. Because of her pushed-in face, her snores were loud.

She'd waddled around for four hours and now didn't even have the energy to mooch when Louis and Angelique ate dinner.

•

Business was steady after that, with three or four customers a day. Some asked for a daily booking because exercise was important and a routine kept you sane. Louis gave these customers a 15 percent loyalty discount. If somebody called and asked for one of the prebooked times, Louis would mention the special deal and the fact that prebooking meant you were never disappointed.

This way, five days into his new business, Sweet Pea was pretty much booked solid.

Angelique's depression had completely lifted by then. She spent a lot of time watching hairstyling videos on YouTube because Louis told her it was important to *keep improving your skills* even during a business slowdown. Louis himself no longer walked Sweet Pea because he didn't want to give up the potential income.

During the second week of the lockdown, Louis got a scare. Something landed on him in the middle of the night like it had dropped from the ceiling.

He woke with a gasp, clutching the pillow and blinking into the darkness.

On the news that day he'd seen a report about animals taking over the empty streets in towns and villages around the world. Sheep and goats roamed freely, eating out of gardens and trimming hedges. One place in South America had been invaded by llamas. In big locked-down cities, hungry rats were forced to venture out even in daylight. There wasn't enough food now that people weren't throwing garbage around.

But it wasn't a rat on his bed. Or a sheep, or a llama. It was Sweet Pea. She kissed Louis' astonished face.

"How did you get up on the bed, Sweet Pea?"

Louis kneaded her and felt not a round body, but a solidly oblong one.

•

Any business will have peaks and troughs.

In other words, an entrepreneur should expect ups and downs. But the skilled entrepreneur, being *flexible*, will know how to *troubleshoot* in the down times and not only survive, but flourish.

Sweet Pea was thirteen years old — two years older than Louis. In dog years, that meant she was sixty-eight. Louis' grandma, whom he hadn't been able to visit because of the virus, was sixty-seven. That meant that Sweet Pea, like Grand-Mère, was an old lady.

So Louis shouldn't have been surprised the morning he approached Sweet Pea on his bed (she usually joined him sometime in the night now). She took one look at the leash and rolled over onto her back, showing Louis her well-toned furry belly. That's what dogs did to say, "You are the boss of me, I know. But I really, really don't want to do what you are asking me to do."

Louis picked her up and set her gently on the floor. She rolled onto her back again and gazed at him with pleading eyes.

Louis sighed. "You've had enough, haven't you, Sweet Pea? You're tired."

Sweet Pea's tail swished back and forth across the carpet.

His regular 7:30 a.m. customer was Reo from upstairs, a kid two grades ahead and two feet taller, a track-and-field star. He was probably the person who had most tired Sweet Pea out. He'd probably made her run!

Rather than cancel by phone, Louis decided to meet Reo, because there was a chance that once Sweet Pea was out of the apartment, she'd change her mind.

Louis carried her to the lobby. Reo was already there in his shorts, running shoes, and face mask, stretching his long legs. He had his hair in a sumo-style ponytail that Louis had never seen on him before. Normally his hair wasn't long enough.

"There's a problem," Louis said. He set Sweet Pea down. She rolled onto her back. "See? She doesn't want to go out."

"I'll carry her," Reo said. "I'm carrying her half the time anyway. I just need to get out."

Reo put the money in Louis' envelope, gathered Sweet Pea in his arms and held her to his chest. She was already wagging like crazy so Louis opened the door for them, handing Reo the poop bag as he and Sweet Pea jogged off.

After breakfast, Louis went back down to wait for Reo to come back. The next customer, Danila, sat behind him at school — when there was school. It seemed a hundred years ago. She walked Sweet Pea with her mom and little sister, Mimi.

Louis just couldn't see them lugging Sweet Pea around for an hour. And he couldn't see Sweet Pea enjoying being carried so much. He'd have to cancel.

In fact, Sweet Pea looked a little queasy when Reo returned and set her on the floor of the lobby.

"Thanks, man," Reo said.

Danila and her family came down the stairs wearing masks. Reo moved six feet away to let them pass. It was automatic now. Nobody had to think about it.

Like Reo, Mimi had her hair gathered in a ponytail on the top of her head to keep it out of her eyes, but hers spurted like a fountain. Danila wore a headband. She smiled shyly at Louis.

Their mother, in a bandanna, had a tired, worried face like most of the parents these days. Hers was a little swollen, like she'd been crying.

Louis told them, "I'm sorry, but Sweet Pea needs a day off."

"Are you sick, Sweet Pea?" the girls asked, which prompted the dog to mooch some pats.

"She's just tired."

"Sweet Pea needs a baby carriage," Mimi said.

Louis laughed, but it was a good idea. "Do you have one?"

"We do," their mother said. "It's in the storage room. Wait a minute and I'll go get it."

She came back with a foldable stroller, opened it and brushed it off. "You don't mind a little dust, do you, Sweet Pea?"

Right away the girls started arguing about who got to push first, the way they always argued about holding the leash. Louis was still grinning his head off over the stroller. When Danila noticed, she looked embarrassed.

"Fine," she told her little sister. "You go first."

"I guess if anyone says Sweet Pea isn't walking," their mom said, "we can say we're taking her out for a poop."

Louis pulled a bag out of his pocket. "Show them this."

"It's our license!"

They all laughed.

When their mom took out her money, Louis lowered his voice, the way they did on TV when people were making deals. "Listen. No charge if I can keep using the stroller."

The mom gave him a sidelong look from her swollen eyes. "Is your mom working?"

"No."

She put the money in the envelope as usual. "You can keep the stroller *and* the money. My husband still has a job."

"Bye, Louis!" the girls called on the way out.

Their mother paused and studied Louis for a moment. "How come your hair looks so good when everybody else is a fright?"

"My mom's a hairdresser."

"Lucky you."

•

Saved from the *entrepreneurial trough* thanks to a stroller! Sweet Pea spent the rest of the day perambulating around the neighborhood in comfort. She would whine when she wanted to get down and read a pee-mail message on a lamppost or a tree, then add her reply.

At the same time, Louis knew that this business opportunity would be short-lived. Soon they'd lift the lockdown. People would be able to go out again without a pet.

The savvy entrepreneur is always looking for ways to *expand and diversify.* That day, almost every customer commented on Louis' neat hair. Everybody else was as shaggy as a llama.

"Too bad your mom can't do house calls," somebody joked.

Louis had returned to the apartment to find Angelique in front of the computer watching another video. In it, a stylist was demonstrating a wisping technique on a model.

Louis stood watching for a minute.

He thought of Zoom church, which Angelique claimed was only half as good as actual church, but better than no church at all.

•

Feeling shaggy? Looking rough?
GET A ZOOM HAIRCUT!
Our live stylist and live model will lead you through
the process with professional equipment
(fully sterilized)
delivered to your door.
Why not look your best once more?
(Okay, your *almost* best!)
BOOK NOW!

He didn't ask to be paid in advance. At Hair by Angelique, you paid after. Louis' mom charged $45 for a haircut in person, so would only charge $30 for a Zoom cut. In the end, it worked out the same because anybody who could, tipped generously.

Louis took the bookings, wrote them in the Hair by Angelique section of the appointment scribbler, boiled the scissors, combs and clips, dried and wrapped them in plastic (while wearing rubber gloves and a mask). He dropped the tools off at the door of each client's apartment (they were called "clients" in a salon), knocked, then hurried back to be the live model for the Zoom haircut. In between, he picked up and dropped off Sweet Pea in the lobby.

After two days he was as exhausted as Sweet Pea. Sweet Pea herself was getting tired of the stroller rides. Now as she was wheeled out of the building, she cast Louis a mournful glance.

"Do I have to go out again?" it seemed to say.

Louis sat on the swivel desk chair in front of the computer. He waved to Sam, who was sitting in front of his computer in apartment 3B. Sam was in grade three, freckled and blue-eyed. He waved back skeptically and let out a puff of air that ruffled his dirty-blond bangs.

Angelique draped Louis in a towel. Sam's mother draped him. Louis only saw her hands.

Sam looked up at his mom. "But I don't want a boy's haircut."

"Don't worry," Angelique reassured him. "We're not going to cut your hair like Louis'. I'm just using him to show your mom what to do."

Louis understood why Sam was worried. Even though Angelique was barely trimming his hair, each time she demonstrated, Louis' hair was a fraction of an inch shorter. After a few more cuts he'd be as bald as Conner's dad.

"No!" Sam covered his head with his arms.

Louis glanced at the clock. Ten minutes until he had to collect Sweet Pea from the lobby.

"Listen, Sam," he said. "Can you meet me back here in fifteen minutes? I have a surprise."

"A surprise?" Sam perked up.

Louis waved and shut off the camera.

"What now?" Angelique asked.

"Maman?" he told her. *"The customer is always right."*

•

Fifteen minutes later, when Sam and his mom Zoomed in for their appointment, a different model waited on the chair, her moppy hair curtaining her pushed-in face.

"Sweet Pea!" Sam shrieked.

Angelique took up the spray bottle and misted Sweet Pea's head. Sam's mom misted Sam's.

Angelique parted the dog fur into sections with the comb, securing each one with clips. Sam's mom followed along.

"You're so cute, Sweet Pea!" Sam cooed. "Now we'll be twins!"

Sweet Pea wagged and sighed with happiness.

Finally, she got to stay home, too.

6

APARTMENTS
2A & 2C

The Two Harriets

They — Jessica, her teenaged brother Jacob and their parents, Nancy and Alan — baked bread. The first batch didn't rise, so they rolled it out flat and baked accidental crackers instead.

A lot of accidental crackers.

They cleaned everything, even the light fixtures. Alan stood on a chair, unscrewed each globe and passed it down to Jacob, who shook the dead flies onto a sheet of newspaper.

Jacob kept the flies. He transferred them to a cigar box that he kept on the dresser in the room he shared with Jessica, a curtain separating their two sides. When Jessica asked what he planned to do with the flies, he said, "Eat them, of course."

He lived to gross her out.

They learned to play the one musical instrument they had in the apartment — a plastic recorder. Jacob refused because he said spit collected inside it and could transmit the virus. Instead, he assembled a drum set from pots and pans and bowls. Then they recorded themselves playing and singing "Oh, Susanna!" to send to Jessica and Jacob's grandparents.

They got a big shock when they played it back. It sounded like a garbage truck backing over a trio of howler monkeys.

They — just Jessica and her parents this time — learned to crochet. Together they made half an afghan, which they abandoned when the weather warmed up and they ran out of yarn.

Jacob wouldn't crochet, or give them a reason why not. He said it was "obvious."

"Are you gender-stereotyping, young man?" Nancy asked.

They finished a 2,000-piece jigsaw puzzle of the night sky. Jacob worked on Orion's belt. So his pants wouldn't fall down, he said.

They drew pictures and because none of them was a very good artist (Alan's people had no necks), they reused the paper when they taught themselves origami.

They reread all the books in the apartment. They didn't actually own that many books, being not only avid library users, but four people working and "going to school" in a two-bedroom apartment where shelf space was limited. Jessica still had a few treasured favorites: *Frog* and Toad, *Charlotte's Web, Harriet the Spy*. Jacob: *One Hundred Best Fart Jokes*.

They could borrow ebooks from the library, of course, but the point of these activities according to Nancy and Alan was to keep their kids, and themselves, off their computer and phones for at least part of the day. But as those days got longer and their tempers shorter (Jacob's, mainly), Nancy and Alan gave up trying to force their kids to do offline things. Also, there were so many wonderful activities, like square dancing and yoga (Jacob: "Kill me now!") that they could only do watching YouTube videos.

"We should all learn a language," Nancy suggested at dinner one night. They were having Jessica's favorite: Moroccan chicken with raisins.

"What language?" Alan asked, passing around the bottomless basket of hard, half-burnt crackers.

"How about Mandarin?"

"Seriously?" Jacob said. "That's, like, the hardest language in the world."

"Maybe," Nancy said. "That's why I think we should all learn it *together*."

Jacob coughed and sent cracker crumbs spewing across the table.

"Ick," Jessica said. "Did you just infect us?"

"I'll learn Mandarin with you, sweetheart," Alan said.

Jacob refused, shaking his head of overgrown hair. He looked like an Irish setter now. Both he and Jessica had inherited the red from their dad.

Nancy said, "You have friends who speak Mandarin, Jacob. You could talk to them."

"They would laugh me out of the room if I tried to speak Mandarin. Not that I'll ever be in the same room with them again *ever in my life*."

"Oh, honey, you will."

"When? Next year? By then my social development will be stunted."

"You're already stunted," Jessica told him. She turned to Alan and Nancy. "He's collecting dead flies. He says he's going to eat them."

Alan looked up from his dinner. "He's *what*?"

"Actually, *you're* eating them." Jacob pointed at Jessica's plate.

"I'm going to throw up!" she said, pushing it away.

"Jacob, I know this is hard," Nancy said, "but we'll get through it as a family."

"I'm fifteen! I don't need a family! I need a peer group!"

This sort of argument occurred whenever their parents introduced an activity to distract them from what was happening in the world. Their reasonableness eventually wore Jacob down, as usual. He said he'd learn a second language, but one he chose himself.

•

Jessica missed her friends, too. She knew most of the kids in the building. They went to the same school —

when there was school — and played or hung out in the playground just behind the apartment building.

Back when they were allowed to go out for walks, they waved to each other from across the street. They texted and phoned, Skyped, Zoomed or FaceTimed. But after a while, Jessica lost interest and burrowed deeper into her family cocoon. Since they were all stuck at home, what was there to talk about anyway?

The one girl in the building Jessica didn't know had moved into the next-door apartment only a couple of months before the virus hit. She didn't go to the neighborhood school or hang out in the playground. She was Deaf and went to Deaf school. Her dad was Deaf, too. Sometimes Jessica saw them out on the balcony talking with their hands. It looked pretty cool.

The girl's name was Meena. Nancy found it out when she met the mother, who was hearing, in the hall shortly after they moved in.

One day Jacob was counting his fly collection, which he did whenever he wanted to drive Jessica out of their room. He yanked back the curtain and glared from under all his hair.

"You ate two of my flies. There are only sixteen now."

"You're making me *sick*!" Jessica screamed.

She stormed out, all the way to the balcony, which was about as far away from Jacob as she could get.

Meena's balcony door slid open and she stuck her head out. Jessica smiled and waved. Meena's eyes widened and she ducked right back inside, though her hand did flutter in Jessica's direction before the door closed again.

Shy, Jessica thought.

•

After just one Mandarin lesson, Alan switched to Spanish. Jacob said there were twenty-three languages on the app he'd downloaded. He wanted to choose carefully, but at the moment was trying to decide between Icelandic and Swahili.

Jessica started learning ASL, American Sign Language.

Nancy said, "Jessie, that's smart. You can practice with Meena next door."

"Muy bien, Jessica," Alan agreed.

The first thing she taught herself was finger spelling. It turned out that you could talk to somebody in ASL simply by spelling all the words. And J was her favorite letter! You stuck out your baby finger and drew a J.

It was like a secret code. Like something spies would use. If you knew ASL, you could talk to your friend on the other side of the classroom and nobody would know what you were saying. You could gossip and cheat on tests (not that she would!). It would be better than passing notes or secretly texting, because a note or a phone could be confiscated.

Would they ever go to school again?

Jessica practiced in the mirror, smiling. She wandered around the apartment finger spelling objects.

Lamp. Table. Computer. Mom. Dad. Brother. Jerk. Fly-eater.

Jacob ripped out his earbuds and said, "What's the *matter* with you?"

She printed out the ASL alphabet and, feeling shy herself, stepped outside. Meena's balcony was about ten feet away.

Even if Meena could hear, it would be weird to call her name when they'd never properly met. How to get her attention?

Jessica remembered then that Meena's mother could hear. She went back inside for the recorder, which had been left on the shelf when the family discovered just how unmusical they were. She sat on the patio chair and began to play "Oh, Susanna!" tunelessly.

It worked! The third time through, Meena's mom stuck her head out the door with an annoyed expression on her face. Jessica leapt up.

"Hi! Is Meena home?" Duh! Where else would she be?

She smiled. "You're Jessica, right? I'll go get her."

Meena appeared a moment later. Her curly black hair was in pigtails with barrettes to hold it out of her eyes. Combs restrained Jessica's red mop.

Today, Meena looked more curious than shy.

When Jessica finger spelled *H-I*, the curiosity became surprise. Meena's hands flew into the air and began moving fast. Meena was a very talkative person!

Meena saw that Jessica wasn't following her. She stopped and waved. She spelled *H-I* and waved again.

"Oh. That's obvious." Jessica waved, too, and Meena dissolved in a happy laugh. She had a dimple on one cheek but not the other.

Jessica pointed to herself and slowly spelled out her name.

Meena placed her fingers just in front of her chin, like she was shielding it, then let that hand fall back into the palm of the other hand. And again, nodding and smiling. Jessica still didn't get it, so Meena went and got her phone.

She typed something and stretched her arm out so Jessica could read it. *Good.*

Now Jessica had two real ASL words she didn't have to spell: *Hi* and *good.*

Before they finished talking, she had learned *yes, no, please, Deaf, hearing.* And when Meena hooked her index fingers together one way, then the other, Jessica could actually understand it.

It wasn't random. There was a beautiful logic to it.

It was the sign for *friend.*

•

The second day that the two girls met on their side-by-side balconies, Meena's mother came out with her. Meena looked most like her mom, who was South Asian. Her father was tall and blond.

"You probably noticed that Meena didn't spell her name out," her mom told Jessica. "This is her name.

The letter M, for Meena, tapped twice on her cheek where her dimple is."

Meena's mom paused to sign what she'd said to Meena. Meena signed *yes*, and repeated her name, which in ASL was technically *M-M dimple*.

"When a hearing person enters the Deaf community, you have to wait to receive a name. The community bestows it on you. It's an honor. Meena has given you a name."

"Really?" Jessica said. She did feel honored.

Meena grinned and showed her. There was baby finger J brushing her chin twice.

As Jessica repeated it, Meena pointed to Jessica's hair. The second sign meant *red*. M-M dimple: *Meena*. J-J red: *Jessica*.

Both girls laughed and laughed. Then Meena pulled her phone out of her pocket and wrote: *Can we text*?

•

Now whenever Jacob irritated her, which happened several times a day, Jessica fled to the balcony. Sometimes Meena was already there. They both hung out there more often now. If Meena was inside, Jessica would text *Come out*. Meena texted Jessica, too.

But Jessica didn't want only to text. She really wanted to learn ASL. To speak to Meena she used a mixture of miming, finger spelling and actual ASL words that Meena had taught her, or that she'd looked up herself on the app. She probably communicated at the same level as Nancy in Mandarin, or Alan in Spanish, or Jacob in Serbo-Croatian (he had given up on Icelandic and Swahili).

Somehow they seemed to communicate perfectly! When Jessica thought back on their conversations, she even remembered them as that — conversations. It was like when Nancy and Alan forced her and Jacob to watch a movie with subtitles, or in black and white. In her memory it was always in English and in color.

One afternoon Jessica texted Meena. When she appeared, Jessica signed, *"What are you doing?"* She loved that sign with its pinching fingers.

And Meena answered, *"Reading."*

Jessica actually hadn't learned that sign yet, but she got it instantly: Meena brushed two fingers against the flat of her hand twice, like the gaze of a pair of eyes scanning a page.

Meena disappeared and returned with the book she was reading, *Harriet the Spy.* The Harriet on the cover looked shaggy and sloppy, like she was sheltering in place, too, dressed in her red hoodie, spy notebook tucked under her arm.

"That's one of my favorite books ever!" Jessica gushed, babbling on until she caught herself and began to finger spell, *"F-A-V-O—"*

Meena already understood. She was nodding and signing, *"Good."*

Meena made the H sign. Then she pointed one finger at herself and two at Jessica.

H-1: *Meena.* H-2: *Jessica.*
Harriet 1 and *Harriet 2.*

By then, Jessica knew that ASL used more than the fingers and hands. It involved the whole face.

A sneaky look crossed Meena's. She glanced furtively around, then signed something else, which Jessica understood as perfectly as if she'd shouted it out.

"Let's be spies!"

•

Both girls started carrying notebooks to record their observations, just like Harriet. Luckily, their apartments were at the front of the building, so they could monitor who came and went, and when. If they woke up early enough, they also watched the hospital workers at morning shift change. In the evening, after the pot banging that both families participated in, the two Harriets would stay behind to sign to the other where they'd hidden their daily reports.

These were the day's observations torn from their spy books and hidden around the building — under doormats, behind lobby plants, in the laundry room. They could have texted, but that wouldn't have been authentically Harriet.

Like the hospital workers, Harriets 1 and 2 spied in shifts.

Together, they were able to monitor what happened most of every day.

6:55 Nurse from 3A crosses street for work. Everybody 6 feet apart. Workers start coming out. They look tired. New shift goes in.

7:18 Old lady leaves building with shopping buggy. Striped socks.

7:21 Dad on 3rd floor comes out on balcony to smoke.

7:40 Ambulance.

7:55 Ambulance.

8:25 Building manager sweeps front walk. Picks up garbage with tongs. Candy wrappers. Cigarette butts! A face mask. (Yuck!) Black and white cat comes out. Rolls around on sidewalk.

8:32 Ambulance.

8:40 Ambulance.

9:10 3rd floor Dad smokes again. (He smokes too much!)

9:15 Old lady comes back. Full buggy. Toilet paper!

9:16 Family from 2nd floor leaves right after. Mom, baby in stroller, two boys. Boys acting weird. Why??? Scratching themselves.

9:27 Boy from 1st floor leaves to walk dog.

9:32 Ambulance.

9:43 UPS delivery van. Man in brown buzzes, leaves package. Small box. Books? Drops tissue on ground and doesn't notice. (Yuck!)

9:45 4th floor man, bald. Blue bathrobe, plastic sandals. Picks up parcel.

11:01 2nd floor family comes back. Boys still acting weird.

11:04 Ambulance.

11:05 Spy takes break ...

•

"Where are you going?" Nancy asked the first time Harriet 2 got caught sneaking out to find Harriet 1's report.

"Just downstairs. I'll wear my mask. Meena left something for me." Of course she didn't call her Harriet!

"Left what?"

"A letter," Jessica said.

That excuse completely satisfied Nancy. "I wish Jacob could get off his phone like you do."

Harriet 2 skipped off. What a great spy!

Back on their balconies, they pored over the details of each other's report. Harriet 2, who knew everybody, filled in some blanks for Harriet 1. The names of the tenants, what they did, the names of their pets. The black-and-white cat, Bill, belonged to Mr. Chu, the building manager. Sweet Pea was the dog.

Harriet 2 used the ASL dictionary, but she knew a lot of words by heart now. She finger spelled Mrs. Watts. Signed *old*. It was like pulling on a long beard. She looked up the sign for England, which was where Mrs. Watts had come from centuries ago. She was like the building's grandmother.

"Grandma," she signed.

Meena nodded.

They wondered why Conner's dad smoked so much. They speculated on whether or not the bald man from the fourth floor ever got dressed, and what was in all the packages he ordered. Maybe he was building something.

Maybe a D-R-O-N-E? Harriet 1 made the question mark with her elastic eyebrows.

Maybe he was a spy, too, working for a sinister organization!

And what was up with the boys from the second floor? Harriet 2 looked up "twins."

"What's wrong with them?" Harriet 1 signed. *"Do they have fleas?"*

They laughed.

The two Harriets often noticed different things. Harriet 1 included tiny details: the patterns on people's socks, if something fell out of somebody's pockets. She seemed to have Super-Vision. She was fascinated to learn about the arguments from 3C, or the building manager's opera music warbling right below her, which Harriet 2 reported on.

Often people talked in front of the building, loud enough to hear because they were standing six feet apart. Harriet 2 transcribed what they were saying for Harriet 1, but most of the conversations were boring. Who got laid off, or sick. What was, or wasn't, in the store. Toilet paper was an obsession. Also flour. (*Boring* in ASL was a finger twisted on the side of the nose, like nose-picking. Jessica revenged herself on Jacob with it, signing, *"Boring, boring, boring,"* whenever he spoke to her.)

The only remotely interesting incident was when a budgie escaped from one of the apartments. Harriet 2 heard somebody outside singing "Happy Birthday" over and over. She looked down on a middle-aged woman holding a cage, the door open.

"Have you seen a blue budgie?" the woman called when she noticed Harriet 2 on the balcony.

Harriet 2 shook her head just as Harriet 1 stepped out. Harriet 2 finger spelled *B-I-R-D*.

Harriet 1 pointed to where it was perched in a tree.

"There it is," Harriet 2 called down, pointing, too.

Then both spies watched as the woman lured the budgie back by cooing, "Namaste, Namaste," over and over.

•

At dinner Nancy announced with a grin, "I have something to tell you all."

Jessica and Jacob shrank down, expecting some new activity.

Instead she said, taking quite a long time to get the sounds out, *"Woah djow Nan-cee. How she woo!"*

"Huh?" said Jessica and Jacob.

"I just said '*My name is Nancy. Good food,*' in Mandarin," she told them, beaming.

"In your dreams," Jacob muttered.

Alan clapped. "My turn. *Me nombray es Alan. Bwena comeeda.*"

Nancy clapped, then Jessica did. They all turned to Jacob, who said something that sounded like, *"Eeny meeny ack steen kook."*

"What's that supposed to be?" Jessica asked.

"Pashto. They speak it in Afghanistan."

"It's not Pashto," Jessica said.

"It is. It's a well-known Pashto fart joke."

"It's not!"

"Like you'd know Pashto if you heard it. Let's hear your language then."

Jessica's ASL had improved so much by then that she could understand some of Meena's conversations with her dad on their balcony. She lifted her hands in the air now and let them sign every word she knew. *Yes. No. Hi. Nice. Who? What? Learn. What are you doing? Good. Spell. Red. Blue. Dimple. Friend. Deaf. Hearing. School. How many? Door mat. Plant. Laundry Room. Front. Back. Over. Under. Big. Small. Like. Don't like. Old. England. Grandma. Reading. Bird. Breakfast. Dinner. Mom. Brother. Father. Bathroom. Socks. Ambulance. Toilet paper. Sick. Twin. Flower. Bird. Cat. Flea ...*

Her family gaped.

Jessica finished with: *I'm a good spy!*

•

After dinner and pot banging, the two Harriets told each other where they'd hidden their reports. Both slipped out to retrieve them. Then they met on the balcony again. Harriet 1 got back first because Harriet 2 had left her report right under Harriet 1's doormat.

Harriet 1 made the beard sign that meant *old*. She signed, *"Where's Mrs. Watts?"* then held up two of Harriet 2's reports — yesterday's and today's.

Harriet 2 read her reports, written by Harriet 1, and confirmed it. Mrs. Watts hadn't left the building in two days. Normally she went to the store every morning, probably for the exercise.

Harriet 1 signed that Harriet 2 should investigate. She signed *door*. It was one of the more obvious ones: two hands held palm out like double doors, one opening. She signed *knock*. Also obvious.

"*Now* where are you going?" Nancy called. "You just went out."

"I'll be right back."

"Jessie? *Where* are you going?"

Jessica beat it down the two flights of stairs, putting on her cloth mask as she went. She knocked on Mrs. Watts's door.

No answer. Maybe she was in the bathroom.

She waited a minute, then knocked again louder.

"Mrs. Watts? Are you there?" she called.

Nothing. When Jessica turned, Meena was on the stairs. It seemed strange to see her there instead of on the balcony. Her eyes looked huge over her mask. She pointed to the door across the hall from Mrs. Watts's — the building manager's.

Jessica knocked. She stepped six feet back.

When Mr. Chu opened the door, his cat shot out into the hall. "Bill! You get back in here!"

Jessica blurted, "Do you have Mrs. Watts's phone number? Can you call and see if she's okay? She hasn't gone out in two days."

"Jessie? What's going on?"

It was Jacob, standing higher on the stairs, a safe distance from Meena, but maskless.

Mr. Chu came striding across the hall with his phone to his ear. He knocked twice on Mrs. Watts's door, gave up and slipped the phone in his back pocket. He shooed Jessica away.

Out came his jangling key ring. He opened the door and called, "Gladys?"

A faint groan sounded from inside.

Jacob looked from Meena to Jessica. "*How* did you know?"

Before Jessica could tell Meena what Jacob had said, Mr. Chu let the door close again.

"Go home," he ordered. Then he took the phone out again and dialed 9-1-1.

•

They watched from the balcony — Jessica and her family, Meena and hers. Meena was signing to her parents so fast that Jessica knew she must be telling them what had happened.

"How terrible," Nancy said when she saw the paramedics below.

They didn't bother with the ambulance. They just ran across the street like astronauts in pale yellow jumpsuits, rubber gloves, goggles under the face shields, masks over their nose and mouth. The stretcher glided along between them.

Mr. Chu opened the door of the building to let them in.

Nancy phoned a few other people in the building to tell them Mrs. Watts was sick. Soon everybody on the hospital side came out to watch as the old woman, strapped down on the stretcher, oxygen mask over her face, was wheeled down the walk.

After a long solemn hush came a sob. Jessica had never heard anything but laughter from Meena. Now she was bawling her head off, her parents comforting her. Meena broke away and turned to Jessica with a fierce expression on her face. Her hand went up to her mouth, then flew into the air like she was flinging something. Again, again.

"Yell!" she was telling Jessica.

"MRS. WATTS, YOU'RE GOING TO BE OKAY!!!" Jessica called.

She started off a chorus. More voices rained down.

"WE'RE ROOTING FOR YOU, GLADYS!"

"HANG IN THERE!"

Jacob tore inside, came back with the recorder and started blasting it. The pot lids banged again.

"WE LOVE YOU, GLADYS!"

By the time the stretcher reached the other side of the street, it sounded like the whole building was cheering Mrs. Watts on.

Mrs. Watts must have heard them because she made a sign. One hand lifted slowly in the air, fingers curled. Up went her thumb.

125

7

APARTMENT
3A

The Incredible Escaping Bra Man

If you lived with a superhero, you lived with *sound effects*.

They were hardest for Claudia to bear in the morning, when Spidey Max's high-pitched *eeeeee* woke her way too early. When he levitated three feet in the air and — *whoosh* — landed in a crouch on the bed, grabbed the skipping rope tied to the headboard (his Spidey line) and leapt to the floor with a *thud*.

When he pretend-swung — *weeeeee!* — across the imaginary bottomless gap between bed and door, then reached for the next Spidey line tied to the knob (the belt of Syl's bathrobe).

These lines were all over the apartment, Spidey Max's means of locomotion, tripping hazards for everybody else.

If Claudia was lucky, she fell back to sleep after he left the room, but she was mostly not lucky because

he was only going to the bathroom. He came swing-
ing back — *weeeeee!* Then Spidey Max would pull his
Spider-Man action figure from wherever it was buried
in the bed and begin acting out Spidey adventures, all
of which involved a steady stream of *BAMs* and *POWs*.

If Moma had worked the night shift, Claudia worried that the sound effects would wake her, too.

She got up and made breakfast.

Spidey Max couldn't just come to the table and sit
down on his chair. No. He had to crouch-hop Spidey-style
from Spidey line to Spidey line, then onto the seat where,
squatting, he ate his bowl of mummified bugs and flies
(aka Sugar Puffs).

Spider-Man Hallowe'en costume, Spider-Man underpants, Spider-Man sheets, T-shirts, pajamas, lunch
box, baseball cap, coloring books, action figures …

The whole Spidey thing was out of control! Claudia
would have loved to take a big can of Raid and blast the
Spidey part of her little brother away.

Instead, she streamed another Spider-Man cartoon
on the computer to keep him quiet until Moma woke
up.

•

Moma was short for Mom-A, or Mom-Aisha. Moms
was Mom-S, or Mom-Sylvia. Spidey Max still called her
Moms, but Claudia had switched to Syl when she got
older. It was easier than explaining the whole Moma/
Moms thing to friends.

A year and a half ago Syl got sick. Max was only four at the time, Claudia ten and a half. Moma broke the news at a family meeting with Syl beside her on the sofa, looking embarrassed, rubbing the back of her neck where her hair was shaved close. Claudia loved that place on Syl, loved to brush the tips of her fingers against the prickly bristles.

Moma was a nurse so she explained everything that was going to happen to Syl in a calm and reassuring way, but she was also honest.

"Moms will be very sick and fragile for a long time. A couple of years." She looked at Syl and squeezed her hand.

Syl said, "When I go into the hospital for the transplant, I'll need you two to be patient with each other and helpful to Moma. Right, Max?"

Max was lying on the floor parallel parking his Matchbox cars, making engine sounds with his lips. He nodded.

Obviously, he didn't get that their lives were falling apart.

"Claudie-Baby?" Syl said. "Are you okay with all this? Need a hug?"

Claudia did, but she shook her head. She was afraid she'd start to cry.

Moma explained chemotherapy in a way Max could understand. "It will kill all the bad cells in Moms' blood. Then she'll get new bone marrow so she can make healthy blood cells again."

Max said, "Pow! Bam!" and everybody laughed.

A few months after that they moved from their town-house to this apartment building because it was right across from the hospital. They felt squeezed together with Claudia and Max in the same bedroom, but it was only temporary. Once Syl was better, they'd move again.

The night before the transplant, they all crossed the street to visit Syl. It would be the last time Claudia and Max would see her for a long time. Until the new bone marrow was up and running, even something like a cold was dangerous to her. And kids were so germy, especially little kids.

Max started running around Syl's bed, *BAMing* and *POWing*.

"What are you doing, you wacky kid?" Syl asked him.

"Killing the bad cells!"

They all laughed again, but later, back in the apartment, Claudia threw herself on her bed and sobbed. What if Syl died?

The tears eventually stopped, but for a long time she lay in the dark feeling the fear grow inside her. When Moma was pregnant with Max, her whole body swelled. She said her organs were getting squashed. The fear felt like that to Claudia, like it was crowding out her insides. It grew and grew until it just had to leave her body — a separate being hovering above her while she lay paralyzed on the bed.

Fear with a capital F. It was formless, but had a temperature. *Cold*. It had a weight. *Heavy*.

All those months when Syl was in hospital, Claudia sensed Fear lurking nearby. If she thought of Syl, which she did pretty much all the time, or if she went out on the balcony and looked across at the hospital, Fear would be there, ready to paralyze her again.

Moma took leave from her job at the clinic so that she could help look after Syl. She spent the day at the hospital, then picked up Claudia and Max from school with the Syl Update: So-so day, Okay day, Bad day.

On weekends, Moma would go for a short visit. On Okay days, they would Skype.

"That's not Moms," Max said when he saw Syl for the first time on the screen. "Moms isn't bald. She's not *orange.*"

It was true that she looked different. Not only had her hair fallen out — no more prickles! — her skin had turned a funny color, like she'd washed her face in orange Kool-Aid. Not because she was dying, Moma assured them. These were side effects from the chemo-therapy.

Still, every time Claudia saw Syl's unprickly head and her orange-stained face, she felt Fear creep up behind her …

Finally, Syl came home, though she was still weak and needed a walker to get to and from the bathroom.

Max ran off to the bedroom and changed into his Spider-Man Hallowe'en costume. He dragged along a skipping rope, which he wound around Syl and her chair.

"BAM-BAM! POW!" he hollered. "I'm killing the bad cells!"

Syl said, "You can untie me, Spidey Max. The bad cells are all gone."

"Then why's your hair funny?"

Syl's hair had grown back curly where before it had been straight. So curly it made her look like she could have given birth to Claudia and Max instead of Moma. Syl would never be prickly again.

"I'm going to make sure those bad cells never come back!" Spidey Max told her.

And so a superhero took over the bed across from Claudia's.

It was his way of dealing with what had happened, Moma and Syl explained to Claudia. As Spidey Max, her little brother didn't feel so afraid.

•

Moma quit her old job at the clinic for good and started working at the hospital across the street. It was more convenient. Syl still couldn't work — she was a manager at the city parks department — but she was improving slowly. If she had a doctor's appointment, she usually spent the rest of the day in bed. Claudia helped out with Spidey Max.

By Christmas, Syl said she felt strong enough to drive to see Grams and Gramps, two hours away. Gram-S and Gramp-S. (They'd have to take a plane to see Gram-A and Gramp-A.) They stayed in a hotel because Grams and Gramps lived in a no-kids, no-spiders complex. Also, their apartment was too small.

They made up Spidey carols in the car: *We Wish You a Spidey Christmas*, *We Three Superheroes*, *Spiders We Have Heard on High*.

"On the first day of Christmas my true love gave to me ... a Spider-Man DVD!"

Their bellowing songs filled the car, steamed the windows.

As she sang, Claudia realized something. Fear hadn't been around in ages.

At the time, she thought that it was gone for good.

•

Then, six weeks later, the bedroom door creaked open. Claudia sat up in the dark with the blankets under her chin. She couldn't see it, but she knew it was back. The room felt icy.

In the bed across from hers, Spidey Max slept on.

Fear came to Claudia before most other people were even worried about the virus. Though the radio and the TV reported on it, not many local people had caught it yet. Moma and Syl were worried, though. Syl was still "immune compromised." If she got sick, she could die.

The next morning Moma said at breakfast, "Moms is going to visit Grams and Gramps."

"I want to go, too!" Spidey Max said.

"You have school. Syl will only be there for a few weeks. Just until the danger passes."

Syl came out of the bedroom with a suitcase. She set it down and crouched with her arms open wide. Spidey Max ran to her, but Fear threw an icy arm around Claudia's neck and held her back.

"Claudie-Baby?" Syl said, still crouching.

Claudia broke free. As she hugged Syl, she stroked the feathery back of her neck. It didn't comfort her the way the prickles used to. When Syl was prickly, she seemed so strong.

Moma and Syl drove Claudia and Spidey Max to school. After school, they went home with Juliet, Claudia's friend in Apartment 4B. Moma wouldn't be back from dropping off Syl until later that night.

That was their last play date, but they didn't know it then.

•

One of Claudia's responsibilities during the lockdown was to help keep herself and Spidey Max safe. That meant helping Moma follow "protocols" after work.

If Moma was on the day shift, Claudia and Spidey Max would bang pot lids on the balcony at 7:00 p.m. for Moma and the other frontline workers at the hospital. Then Claudia would hurry downstairs and prop open the back door of the building so Moma wouldn't have to touch the handle. Moma used that door to avoid the lobby, where she was more likely to run into another tenant.

Though Moma wore Personal Protective Equipment

over her scrubs, she insisted on extra precautions. Claudia dropped a bag of clean clothes in the laundry room for her to change into, and detergent so she could throw her hospital scrubs straight into the machine. Back upstairs, Claudia left the apartment door open.

As soon as Moma came in, she heading straight for the shower, disinfecting everything in the bathroom afterward. Only then were Claudia and Spidey Max allowed to get close her.

They had dinner while Skyping with Syl and Grams and Gramps, everybody sharing the non-events of their day. Moma never mentioned what it was like at the hospital. She waited until Claudia and Spidey Max went to bed.

But Claudia couldn't fall asleep, not with Fear squatting on her chest, pinning her down on the mattress. She struggled for breath just like the sick people Moma described to Syl when she Skyped her later. Claudia heard them talking through the wall. Syl begged Moma to quit.

"You're already exhausted. I can see it, hon," Syl told Moma.

"They're desperate for nurses. How could I let them down after they saved your life?" Then she said, "I just wish I could have sent the kids with you."

"Me too. I miss you all so much!"

"They'd be safer away from me. And I worry about Claudia. This is too much responsibility for a twelve-year-old."

Claudia could have dealt with it, if not for Fear. She would be working on her school assignments, forgetting that Moma was risking her life every time she went to work, forgetting that Syl had to live far away from them and that if the virus ever reached her, she would probably die.

But then Fear would sneak up behind her. She'd feel its cold presence, get goosebumps. Her fingers froze on the keys.

An icy whisper. "Check the stats."

Claudia would have to. She'd Google the virus and read the horrifying tally of infections growing by the minute around the world, then escape to the balcony. But it was no better there with an overflowing hospital across the street.

Her friend Danila lived in the apartment above, Jessica one floor down and across. Jessica had made friends with the new girl, Meena, and now they were all learning sign language. That distracted Claudia for a while.

If the girls weren't on their balconies, Claudia sometimes talked to Conner, aka Loudboy, from next door. She didn't use to like Conner. Before, he was always sneering. But he seemed different now.

For one, he actually talked to her without curling his lip. Once, after she helped him with his math, he tossed her a roll of toilet paper from his balcony.

"Are you sure?" Claudia asked.

"Yeah. My dad scored a package yesterday."

"Thanks a lot!"

Soon Claudia began to notice something. If she was talking to one of her friends, a parent would step out on the balcony, too. "Tell your mom thank you," they'd say, just before they pulled their kid back from the railing, farther from Claudia, though they were already more than six feet apart. Once Conner's dad ordered him to come back inside.

Only one person in the building had caught the virus so far — Mrs. Watts from the first floor. Everybody must have thought that the next people to get it would be Claudia's family, because Moma was a nurse.

So Fear, too, was contagious. It followed Claudia out on the balcony, stretched out its invisible arms and closed its icy grip around her neighbors.

All day long Spidey Max annoyed Claudia. If Moma was sleeping, somehow Claudia had to keep him from shouting, *"BAM-BAM! POW!"* He set traps with his Spidey lines, which she tripped on. He licked her and claimed to have poisoned her with his venom.

If only they were allowed to leave the building! He could have yelled all he wanted, run around and tired himself out. But they were forbidden to go outside. Instead Spidey Max swung on his Spidey lines around the apartment, from sofa to coffee table to armchair. He spilled a glass of juice. He broke a lamp.

The day he swung past and accidentally kicked her in the side of the head, Claudia lost it.

"Ow!!! Stop it with that stupid Spidey stuff! Spidey can't save anybody! Don't you realize that? You're just annoying everybody!"

So Claudia turned out to be the one to wake up Moma.

Moma found her crying facedown on her bed. She rubbed Claudia's back. They weren't hugging anymore just in case Moma did catch the virus.

"You're amazing," Moma said. "You're my superhero. We've been living like this for a month and this is the first time you've lost your temper."

A month? Moma had said that Syl would only be gone for a few weeks. Were they going to live inside and apart for the rest of their lives?

Fear pressed down harder.

Spidey Max appeared in the doorway, bare-chested, his Spider-Man T-shirt in his hand. With his wild pom-pom of hair and his scrawny body, he looked like a brown dandelion.

She felt bad for yelling at him.

"I'm sorry, Max," she sat up to say. "You can be Spidey Max if you want."

Max's face squished up. He hurled his shirt, then sank down in bug-shaped ball, arms covering his head.

"Spidey Max? What's the matter?"

Claudia sat next to him on the floor.

"I want Moms," he kept saying. "I have to kill the bad cells."

"Moms is safer where she is, baby," Moma said from the bed.

Claudia thought of something. "Can't Spidey Max help kill the Grown-up Virus instead?"

Max lifted his face, his expression full of scorn. She obviously didn't know the first thing about superhero powers! "Spidey Max kills *bad cells*."

"Okay. Then maybe you can be a new superhero. Come on. Let's get you suited up."

Claudia went to the toy box in the corner. Max followed. Moma chose that moment to slip out of the room to try to get some more sleep. She mouthed, "Thank you," to Claudia and blew her a kiss.

"Your sword," Claudia told Max, pulling a bright orange swim noodle from the box.

Max humphed. "It's a *zapper*!"

"A zapper, then. And look." She held it out at the end of her arm. "Six feet, right?"

He snatched it from her and — *whoosh* — began slashing the noodle, ninja-style.

"Hold on. You're not ready yet."

They went to the front hall, which was as far as the basket of clean laundry had got into the apartment. Claudia pulled out a scrub top and helped him into it. It hung on Max like a green sack.

Thanks to Syl, the super organizer, they easily found what they needed in the labeled tubs in the closet: gloves, swim goggles. Claudia considered a bike helmet, but thought of something better.

In the magnified pictures she'd seen of the virus, it looked like a ball with fluffy red tufts all over it. She sat Max on a chair and got to work with a package of colored hair elastics, using just the red and pink ones. When she was done, she brought him to the mirror.

Though the top of his tufts were brown, he got it.

"Virus head!" he yelled, slashing the zapper around.

Claudia shushed him. "Moma's sleeping."

She added a finishing touch. One of his former Spidey lines became a belt to hold the zapper at his waist. The only thing missing was a face mask, but the box was in Moma's room.

"We have to wait until Moma wakes up."

"I know what to use," Max said.

He ran off to their bedroom and came back waving one of Claudia's bras.

Moma had just bought them — her first bras. She would have died of embarrassment if it wasn't so funny.

Claudia fit a cup over Max's nose and mouth and tied the straps behind his head. He sauntered back to the mirror.

"What's your name, superhero?" Claudia asked.

"BRA MAN!" He began a ninja noodle-twirling dance with sound effects.

"ZAP, ZAP, ZAP!"

He kicked the air. *"Eeeeee!"*

"Shhh!" Claudia tried to say, but it was the first time she'd really laughed since Syl went away.

At dinner, when they Skyped with Syl and Grams and Gramps, Claudia introduced the new superhero living in the apartment.

"Bra Man, show them how you zap the virus."

She held the phone up so they could watch him twirling and ninja-ing in the living room.

"What's that on his face?" Gramps asked.

"Claudie's bra," Syl said, and Gramps howled with laughter, too.

Moma got ready for work. She told Max that he had to take off the bra to eat and brush his teeth and sleep. After she left for her shift, Claudia and Bra Man went out on the balcony with the pot lids to cheer her on.

At bedtime, Bra Man refused to take off the mask. He climbed into bed with all his gear on, hair still tufted.

"Are you sure you can breathe?" Claudia asked him.

"Eeeee!" said Bra Man through the lacy cup.

•

That night, Claudia fell asleep faster than she had in weeks. Usually Fear kept her up, whispering its terrifying "what ifs."

What if Syl catches the virus?

What if Moma does?

What if Max does?

Fear finally gave her a break. She slept peacefully for several hours.

Then, as clearly as if she'd spoken the words aloud herself, she heard, "What if Max *can't* breathe with a bra tied over his nose and mouth?"

Her eyes opened in the dark. She listened.

Nothing.

Claudia sprang out of her bed and over to Max's. It was empty, the covers tossed back.

"Max?"

The bathroom light was on, but no Max. She checked Moma's room. He wasn't in her bed, or under it, or in the closet, or in any of the places he hid as Spidey Max.

"Bra Man? I don't think this is funny!"

She searched the rest of the apartment — behind the furniture, behind the living-room drapes. Fear spattered her with goosebumps.

Then a horrible thought came to her: *What if he went outside?*

"He wouldn't," Claudia said out loud.

Only Moma went out, to work or get groceries, always masked and gloved.

Claudia slid open the door to the balcony and stepped out into the night. The city seemed quieter. Below, where the ambulances and the frontline workers came and went, the hospital glowed, light flooding the street.

A small goggled figure stood there, tufts sticking out all over his head, twirling a bright swim noodle and kicking the air.

"Eeeeee! ZAP, ZAP, ZAP!"

"Max!" Claudia shouted down. "Get back inside right now!"

He craned to look up at Claudia three stories above. "I'M BRA MAN AND I'M PROTECTING EVERY-BODY!"

"No, you're not! It's dangerous! You're not supposed to leave the building!"

This only made Bra Man kick so hard at the virus that he nearly lost his balance. He slashed with the noodle.

Even if she convinced him to come in, he couldn't get back in the building without the keys. Or had he taken them?

She hurried back inside. The spare keys were in the bowl on the hall table. She snatched them up.

That was when she *saw* Fear for the first time.

It was bigger than she'd imagined. Huge! No longer Fear, now it was FEAR, filling the whole hall, blocking her way.

Her breath stopped. All of her did.

Then she pictured Bra Man battling the invisible virus. Twirling and slashing. *"Eeeeee! ZAP, ZAP, ZAP!"* A blur of movement. An *action* figure.

She heard Moma say, "You're my superhero."

Claudia kicked at FEAR, but nothing happened.

She beat it with her fists and screamed, "GET OUT OF MY WAY!"

Surprised, FEAR shrank enough for Claudia to squeeze past. Before she opened the door, she glared over her shoulder at Fear.

Her fear.

"I don't want you here when we get back," she told it. "Or ever."

And in case it didn't get the message, she slammed the door on her way out.

8

Imagine

It started one night in Apartment 3C with Conner's dad muttering to himself as he shifted things around in the freezer. It sounded like he was tossing bricks.

He turned to Conner and Eden at the kitchen table. The stubble on his head reminded Conner of fur rearing on a dog's back.

"Did you two eat all the ice cream?"

"Yup," Eden said.

She was drawing another heart-rainbow-unicorn-thank-you picture to tape onto the balcony window. Practically every window of the whole apartment building was plastered with these happy pictures, displayed to boost the morale of the hospital workers.

Conner was doing math, which was starting to make sense, unlike his dad's moods.

"I risk my life to go shopping and you don't even leave me any ice cream?"

He might have been joking. Then again, maybe not.

"You drank all the beer," Conner pointed out.

Eden, still coloring her rainbow, said, "And you smoked all the cigarettes."

Dad started yelling. Mom, who'd been in the bath, came running, tying her bathrobe around her dripping body.

"Time out, everybody!" she said, hustling Dad away.

"Aw!" Eden threw down her crayon and headed for the bedroom. "Come on, Conner."

Conner stayed where he was.

"You're gonna get it," Eden sang.

After ten minutes or so of arguing in their bedroom, Mom returned alone, her face sagging.

When she saw Conner, she snapped. "I said time out."

"Why do I have to have a time out because he's in a bad mood? When I'm in a bad mood, he doesn't get a time out."

"Because I'm trying to keep things together here!" Mom yelled.

Conner closed the laptop and slipped it under his arm. "Fine. I'm getting out of here."

"Leave the computer. You're on it too much as it is."

"How am I supposed to do my homework?"

But he left it on the table like she asked. She didn't need grief from him, too.

Conner went out on the balcony. Claudia was on hers.

"Hi," he grunted.

"Hi," she grunted back.

•

In 3A, things weren't so great either. Two nights ago Claudia was a superhero for rescuing her brother. You'd think he would be grateful, that he'd return the favor in some way.

When she brought Max a bandanna to use as a face covering so she could have her bra back, you'd think he'd do what she asked.

"That's a Spidey Max scarf. I'm not Spidey Max anymore. I'm Bra Man, protecting everybody from the virus."

Claudia said she'd make him an actual face mask.

"I'm Bra Man. B-R-A M-A-N." So he could spell now.

"Moma!" Claudia yelled.

Bra Man understood that he shouldn't have left the building. He promised never to do it again. Instead, he'd been going out on the balcony to holler and slash the bright orange swim noodle around. Nobody — not their neighbors, not the hospital workers, not the passersby — could miss him. Every one of them saw the bra on his face.

Of course, everybody who knew them would know it was *Claudia's* bra.

She explained this to Moma now.

"Claudie-Baby?" Moma said. "Who's going to know it's your bra?"

"Who else's would it be?"

Moma had huge breasts. Syl's were medium, but she'd taken her underwear with her.

"I understand you're embarrassed," Moma said. "But you shouldn't be. You're maturing."

"Maturing" meant sprouting painful blobs.

When Moma said, "I'll give Max one of my old bras instead," Claudia wanted to curl up and die. Max's *whole head* would fit into one of Moma's bra cups!

"Don't do that! Please!" she begged.

Moma got offended then. "*I'm* not embarrassed about my body. I hope *you're* not."

"Never mind," Claudia said, throwing up her hands.

She thought about phoning Syl, but why bother? She'd say the same thing. Claudia should love her blobs! Ughh! She stomped off to the balcony, which was the only place in the apartment where she could be alone.

She wasn't alone. Conner from next door was on his balcony. For sure *he* would have seen her bra on Max's face.

Conner said hi, then she did.

It was starting to get dark, the sky rosy, like it was as embarrassed as she was. Conner began to talk about school and how much he missed it. This surprised Claudia because even though he was two grades below her, he had a reputation for getting in trouble. The old

148

Conner would have started making fun of her about Bra Man right away.

"Faizabadi's doing Zoom classes, but we only have one computer," he told her. "I can't always go."

"I had Mr. Faizabadi in grade five," Claudia said. "He's the best."

"He is!" Conner said.

She sensed him sidling closer.

"I heard you went out," he said in a low voice.

Claudia looked over at him. His hair was short. He must have had a Zoom cut or been sheared like the twins in 2D. Freckles and pale serious eyes — really serious.

She nodded.

"Nothing happened to you?" Conner asked.

"I was only outside for a couple of minutes. My brother was outside longer. But we're both fine. My mom works at the hospital and she's okay. Louis takes Sweet Pea for a walk every day."

Conner asked, "Do you want to go?"

Claudia drew back. "Where?"

"Out." He pointed beyond the balcony railing, to the streets and apartments of the outside world.

A shiver ran through Claudia.

She was a good girl. Very good. But where did that ever get her?

"When?" she asked.

"Tonight. Late. We have to wait for them to go to bed."

"Them" meant the parents.

Claudia glanced back at Moma in the kitchen getting their lunches ready. She would be on the day shift tomorrow, so home tonight. Claudia wouldn't leave Max alone.

•

Juliet in 4B wasn't mad at Mom and Pops. They never did anything to make her mad.

But, oh, she was so bored!

One day Pops returned from grocery shopping with a present for her — a book from the Free Library down the street. Normally it was jammed with thrillers and romances. He'd brought a few of those home for Mom, to help with her novel. But that day he'd found a "gem." He wiped it down with bleach water.

"I think they'll be canceling Shakespeare in the Park this year. This might make up for it."

He put the tattered paperback in her hands. *Shakespeare's Words of Wisdom*. It was a book of quotations taken from the plays and sonnets.

Claudia from 3A messaged her. *Jule, wanna do something? Conners sneaking out tonight. I think Im gonna go 2.*

Wha?????? She answered.

Fed up. We'll be careful! C is asking some others. Please come or I wont go.

Juliet lay on her bed with *Shakespeare's Words of Wisdom* on her chest. In the other room she could hear

Mom reading out the latest chapter of her terrible novel to Pops.

She opened the book at random and put her finger on a line.

Pleasure and action make the hours seem short.

"You got that right, Willy." There was nothing to do! The hours felt sooo looong! "So, should I go?" she asked out loud.

She closed and opened the book again. Stabbed her finger on the page.

How sharper than a serpent's tooth it is to have a thankless child!

That meant no. What if Mom and Pops woke up and found her gone? They'd be so worried. So disappointed in her.

For several minutes she lay with her eyes closed.

"One more try."

There is nothing either good or bad, but thinking makes it so.

•

Reo answered her ten seconds later, as usual.

Yes!!!

•

In 4A, Danila and Mimi had created a whole city out of painted stones. Dad got them started on the project to keep them busy because Mom was distracted with worry. Auntie Susie was still stuck on the cruise ship and, even though she'd been locked in her tiny cabin all this time, she'd caught the Grown-up Virus. Headache, fever, cough. She could barely get out of bed. It hurt her to breathe.

So middle people got it, too, not just old people like Mrs. Watts. Even kids could be infected. Sometimes their toes turned purple, or they didn't know they had it, which accidentally spread the virus. This was why they all had to stay apart.

Mom was on the phone with Auntie Susie all the time, and with Grandma, and with the government, trying to get them to bring Auntie Susie home. She kept crying to Grandma that if Auntie Susie died, it would be her fault.

"Auntie Susie won't die, will she?" Mimi asked Danila.

Danila said, "No!" But she actually wasn't sure.

At his worksite, Dad filled his pocket with stones and brought them home at the end of every day. Danila and Mimi washed them in the bathroom sink, then left them on the vanity to dry. In the morning they painted them in bright colors and decorated them with rainbows and hearts and flowers. They painted letters to spell out LOVE and STAY SAFE and APART BUT TOGETHER.

Every single stone Danila painted was a wish for Auntie Susie to come home.

The sisters deposited the stones around the building to cheer everybody up. They put a lot of work into the project.

Then Mr. Chu phoned to say he couldn't vacuum properly with rocks all over the place. Could they please pick them up?

"Fine," Danila said.

They decided to keep the flower stones and make a garden. Some of the bigger ones they repainted as houses. Then they asked Dad to bring bigger stones. Then bricks. Also, more paint!

The bricks became apartment buildings, except for the one that they placed horizontally. That was the hospital.

"This is the apartment building we'll live in with Auntie Susie when she comes home," Mimi said. She surrounded it with stone flowers and her Polly Pocket dolls.

Mom came out of the bedroom and stubbed her toe on the hospital. Instantly, her eyes became Laser Zappers.

"I can't take two steps in this place without stepping on a rock!"

She limped to the bathroom and slammed the door. The tap came on full blast to cover the sound of her crying. Danila and Mimi could still hear her. They heard her crying at night, too, when she thought they were asleep.

Crying was the new normal in 4A.

Danila gathered the stones in the hem of her shirt. Mimi did the same. They went out on the balcony and started dropping them over the railing. Nobody was passing by on the street below. They checked.

Meena from 2A must have looked out the window and noticed that it was raining colored stones because she came out on her balcony, looked up at them and shrugged.

"What's up?" she was saying.

"I can't stand this anymore!" Danila shouted down. She grabbed hanks of her own hair and yanked.

Mimi peeked over the railing and goggled her eyes. "Me neither!"

Meena nodded, circling her finger beside her head. She was climbing the walls, too.

•

That night, when Jessica signed to Meena that they were going to sneak out later, Meena texted Danila right away.

•

Jessica agreed to go because of Jacob. He'd asked Mom for a needle and thread, which she delightedly handed over, thinking he was actually going to sew something (as if). Instead, he strung each fly onto a long thread, which he tacked to the ceiling above his bed. He lay there for hours with his arms crossed behind his head, now and then blowing, setting in motion the small swarm above him.

"You are seriously disturbed," Jessica told him. "I can't stand living with you *another minute*!"

•

Of course they invited Louis. He was the only one who had left the building recently. They felt braver in his company.

•

Nobody invited the cave twins from 2D, but they came anyway.

Earlier that day, they Zoom-bombed Doodoo's work meeting. Doodoo and his co-workers were very surprised to see a pair of shirtless cave boys appear on the screen, grunting and scratching under their skinny arms.

"Ooaw-eek!" they crowed in Cave.

"Ivan! Alek!" Doodoo roared.

Who? Ooak and Eek looked at each other and shrugged just before Doodoo burst into their cave like a woolly mammoth on a rampage, grabbed an ear on each of their shaved heads and twisted.

The twins yelled, "OWWW!!!" which is one of the words that is the same in English and Cave.

Doodoo took away the laptop and said they couldn't use it for a month.

After the 7:00 p.m. pot banging, the cave twins stayed out on the balcony to work on their spearheads, which was when they overheard Juliet and Reo talking about escaping.

Ooak pointed to Eek and Eek pointed to Ooak. They both nodded. "Oo!"

155

•

Now here they all were — except for Max and Sam, sleeping safely in their beds, and Jacob, his earbuds jammed in so tight he didn't hear Jessica sneak out.

They gathered in the empty street behind the building, all of them masked. All of them sleepy and nervous, a little afraid. Excited, too.

The twins first — then the others, one by one — lifted the edges of their masks and inhaled the night air.

No cooking odors. No cooped-up body smells. No burning disinfectant.

No city smells either. No car exhaust or garbage from the bins next to the playground. No cigarette smoke from the folks who sat around on the playground benches at night. The playground was behind yellow tape.

There wasn't anybody else. They looked left and right. Not a single person besides them.

Masks replaced, they looked around their circle. Twelve of them, six feet apart, except for siblings. Danila had to bring Mimi, because she'd woken up and threatened to tell. There she was, bedhead and all. The same with Eden, in her pajamas.

For the weeks of the lockdown every one of them had longed to go outside. Not outside on their balconies, which felt like prisons now. *Really* outside. To run farther than ten feet. To kick a ball. To swim. To ride a bike or skip double Dutch. To swing from the monkey bars.

To be in the *actual* world, not just see it on a screen. But now they just stood there.

"What now?" Claudia asked Conner, whose dangerous idea this was.

Conner glanced at Louis, the experienced one.

The eyes over Louis' mask seemed to say, "Go ahead. It's your idea."

Conner said, "Follow me."

He began to walk, hands in pockets, tilting back his head to look up at the mostly darkened apartments. The others fell in beside and behind him, awestruck by the novelty of walking. Of walking in the middle of the street!

"There are so many stars," Juliet said. "I don't think I've ever seen so many."

Reo came up beside her. "Air pollution's way down. In Nepal they saw Mt. Everest for the first time in, like, decades."

His eyes smiled at her above the mask.

Meena began to sign to the girls.

"What's she saying?" Louis asked Jessica.

"She's asking where we're going."

Did it matter? Louis' walks with Sweet Pea were the best part of his day, but they left him feeling lonely. They all envied him his freedom, but what good was it if he couldn't share it?

The Entrepreneur's Bible had left out an important fact. Some things you couldn't sell or buy. Some things were free. And now they were, all twelve of them.

Free.

Ivan and Alek felt the joy first, felt it deep in their DNA. They'd escaped the cave! They went wild, suddenly bursting out in grunts and running in circles, scratching under their arms.

Meena took out her phone. *Whats with those kids?*

"Don't ask me," Jessica signed to her, laughing.

"Come on!" Conner said and he joined in, racing around like that molecule on Mr. Faizabadi's tie, leaping up on curbs, play-bashing into a mailbox.

"Be careful!" Juliet said. She wasn't worried about Conner. She felt a sudden rush of fondness for the mailbox. Hand over her heart, she told it, "Mailbox! I missed you so much!"

Reo was right there at her side again, hand over his heart, too. "Juliet?"

She looked at him. "Yes?"

"Nothing." He stuffed his hands in his pockets and looked away.

Claudia rushed over to a power pole. "I thought we'd never be together again!"

Then all the girls began doing it — proclaiming their love to these ordinary, taken-for-granted things. Manhole covers and stop signs. Parked cars and trees.

Meena held out her hand with her two middle fingers folded down, the letters I, L and Y all in one. *I love you.*

Then everybody signed their love. Reo signed to Juliet and she signed back to him.

"Really?" he asked her.

He was acting as strangely as the twins, Juliet thought.

Then Conner said in a hushed tone, "Look."

Everybody stopped horsing around. Ahead, a pair of glowing eyes stared at them from a dark alley. After a moment, the shadowy form that owned the eyes emerged and lumbered across the street, trailed by two other pairs of eyes. Under the street lamp they became raccoons.

"Numnum!" Ooak exclaimed to Eek.

They'd heard about this on the news. How all over the world, animals were thriving without humans.

"Shhh," Danila said. "Maybe we'll see more."

They walked on, listening, peering all around the darkened streets, aware again of the stars and the quiet.

Until then, they'd been aimlessly following Conner, but now Meena texted to the other girls: *Is this yr school?*

Before them stood a darkened building, squat and concrete, with a sad, flagless flagpole jutting from a pad of cracked concrete out front. It was ugly, but the sight of it thrilled them.

Conner ran over and tried the door. Locked. He cupped his hands around his eyes and gazed through the glass at the long unlit hall, last season's art still stapled to the bulletin board.

The school motto was painted on the wall. *Is it Fair? Is it Safe? Is it Kind?* Why had he never asked himself those questions before?

Reo raced past. He was running around the school.

Under the motto stood the lost-and-found box, lid open, a sleeve hanging out, as though somebody had rooted through it at the last moment before the doors were closed and locked. Look at how much stuff had been lost!

On Reo's next lap, he stopped and looked inside. "I loved this place."

"I love it, too!" Mimi said. "When will we get to go back?"

Before anybody could think how to answer, a siren sounded in the distance, growing louder. Soon the ambulance came into view. It screamed past right in front of them, lights flashing, freezing them in its red strobe.

After it passed, a hollow silence gathered all around them.

"It's never going away, is it?" Mimi said.

"What?" Danila asked her.

"The Grown-up Virus."

"Sure it will," Louis said.

"The thing is," Conner said. "It's not fair. *They* started it." He meant the adults. "And they don't even act like grown-ups."

All of them pictured the adults they lived with losing their tempers. Ivan and Alek covered the ears that Doodoo had twisted. Jessica remembered how Alan had yelled at her and Jacob, "Stop fighting!" way louder than she and Jacob had been arguing. The kids only fought like sisters and brothers. The moms and dads sometimes fought like cats and dogs.

In fact, the kids were doing okay. (Well, Jessica hated Jacob, but even she understood this was temporary.)

Jessica texted Meena what they were saying. *Grown-ups started the problem. They ARE the problem.*

With her pinky on her temple, Meena signed. Then she spelled it out.

"I-M-A-G-I-N-E," Jessica read.

Imagine if we were in charge, Meena meant.

"There would never be a Grown-up Virus," Danila said, "because we wouldn't keep wild animals in cages, so we wouldn't catch diseases from them."

Mimi chimed in, "There wouldn't even be any animals left at the Espisiay."

"The S.P.C.A.," Danila said.

"They would get adopted. And our auntie wouldn't get sick and …. And 'Happy Birthday' would just be for birthdays, not washing hands."

"And there really would be unicorns!" Eden added.

Then Mimi slumped against Danila. "I'm tired."

"Time to go," Conner said.

Time to go *inside*. Forever? Were they going to grow up inside and apart?

Reo brought up the rear to make sure nobody got left behind. They went straight back — past the gloomy buildings and shuttered stores, the graffiti-scarred alleys.

A half a block from their building, they saw a light. From the way it swept the ground, it seemed to be a flashlight.

They looked at each other in a panic. Were somebody's parents on their way to find them?

As they got closer, they saw it was a flashlight. Somebody was sitting in front of the playground. The beam found them.

"You startled me!" she said.

They hadn't heard that voice in a long time.

"Mrs. Watts?" Mimi said.

She shone the flashlight at her own face, so they saw her eyes behind her huge glasses. Everybody from the front side of the building remembered the night the paramedics came, how she had given them that weak thumbs-up sign.

Now she brought a crooked finger to her masked mouth.

"Shhh. You'll wake them." Their parents. "What are you gang of vagabonds doing up in the middle of the night?"

"What's a vagabond?" Conner asked.

"A wanderer."

"We just wanted to go out," Jessica told her.

"We *had* to go out," Conner said.

"We only went to the school and back."

"Don't tell on us."

"I certainly won't," Mrs. Watts said.

"Are you okay now, Mrs. Watts?" Eden asked.

"I'm … splendid. Just weak. But now I have this contraption." With the flashlight she showed them what she was sitting on — a walker with a seat.

"My auntie's got the virus," Mimi told her.

"I hope she recovers soon."

"Me, too!"

Mrs. Watts moved the flashlight over them again. "Which one of you helped me that night?"

Everybody pointed to Meena. *H-E-R-O* Jessica finger spelled for her.

"Thank you," Mrs. Watts said.

"She's Deaf."

"Like this." Jessica showed her the sign for thank you.

"It's like blowing a kiss," Mrs. Watts said. She made the sign to Meena, who shrugged and pointed to Jessica.

"No way!" Jessica said. She texted *U figured it out!!!*

"What are *you* doing out, Mrs. Watts?" Louis asked.

Mrs. Watts chuckled. "Are you going to tell on *me*? I'm sitting and thinking. Thinking about when I was your age, actually. You probably don't believe that I was once a child."

She pulled her mask down and shone the light on herself again.

"You're *really* old!" Eden said.

When Mrs. Watts laughed, they did see a younger her. Brown hair instead of white. A smooth face, not a wrinkled one. A teasing smile.

"A terrible thing happened back then, too. I was afraid, like you are now."

Mimi and Eden moved closer. "What?"

"A war. We weren't locked inside like now, but sometimes? When the bombs fell? We had to go down to the cellar."

"Bombs?"

She nodded.

Jessica took a stab at signing Mrs. Watts's story, miming the shooting and the falling bombs. Then she took out the phone again and texted it.

Meena nodded solemnly as she read.

"It was dark and cold down there," Mrs. Watt told them. "Worse though, sometimes we came back up to find, instead of a shop or a friend's house, a smoldering hole."

"Wow," Louis said. "You lived through that?"

"I did. The thing we were most afraid of was poison gas. It was like this virus. Deadly, invisible. Everywhere we kids went, we had to carry a mask. Even babies had them. Not cloth masks like these. Rubber and canvas masks that covered our whole faces. Hot and smelly and awkward."

"Did the gas come?" Danila asked.

"It didn't, thank goodness."

"Did the war end?" Mimi asked.

"After four years."

"Four *years*?"

She seemed sorry to tell them. "They were hard years. There were shortages. Food shortages, too. But we helped each other through them, like now. Like how you helped me."

"Were you starving?" Eden asked.

"No. We were lucky. We started growing food. Every patch of ground, we dug up and planted. We called them Victory gardens."

As Mrs. Watts was talking, Jessica was still texting to Meena what was being said. Some of it she acted out. Digging a hole, dropping in a seed. A growing plant.

"We didn't only grow food. We grew friendships as we worked. It helped a lot with the fear. The helplessness," Mrs. Watts said. "Anyway, this was a long time ago. I'm only boring you with it to say that you'll get through this, too."

"Thank you," Louis said. The others echoed him, like in church.

They waited for Jessica to finish texting. Meena nodded. She did that pinky thing again. Placed it above one temple and motioned forward.

"She's saying 'imagine,'" Mimi told Mrs. Watts, pleased with herself for remembering.

What Meena did next shocked them all. She marched over to the playground entrance and tore away the yellow tape. Then she stepped right into that forbidden space and began to tear the tape off the equipment, too.

The ground was strewn with wood chips mixed here and there with litter. Meena pointed to where the monkey bars were cemented in the ground. When Mrs.

Watts shone the flashlight on it, Meena scraped away the wood chips with her foot. Her fingers gestured up the pole.

"Yes," Mrs. Watts said. "Peas would work there. Beans, too."

They all imagined it, even the hunter-gatherers. A garden. The monkey bars covered in vines — a green hideout.

Meena went over to the swings and drew an outline around them with her foot. They saw themselves soaring high above the zucchini. Potatoes. Peppers. Cucumbers. Sliding down among the tomatoes. Tending them. Sharing them.

Juliet said, *"There's rosemary, that's for remembrance; pray, love, remember…"*

"What?" Reo said.

Mrs. Watts chuckled. *"And there is pansies, that's for thoughts."*

Meena looked at Jessica, who knew the sign for flowers. Meena nodded and pointed to a place beside the fence.

They would order the seeds tomorrow. But for now they said goodnight to Mrs. Watts.

"Do you need help going back in?" Conner asked her.

She said she'd sit and think a little longer. She shone the light on the door to guide them, waved and watched them go back inside.

Single file. Together, six feet apart.

AUTHOR'S NOTE

In 2020 and 2021, the novel coronavirus, or COVID-19, spread around the globe. Though no country was spared, they were all affected differently. Many areas imposed at least a short-term period during which citizens were asked to remain inside their homes in order to halt the spread of the disease. The policy had various names, such as "lockdown," "sheltering in place," or a "stay at home" order.

I wrote this book early in the pandemic, inspired by the stories I read in the newspaper or on social media about the ingenuity and resilience of children during those frightening months. While some events mentioned are true, the characters and setting are imagined and intended as a tribute to children the world over.

Many thanks to Shelley Tanaka, Allison Matichuk, Ariel Baker-Gibbs and Rachel Wyatt for their wise input and kind support.

CAROLINE ADDERSON is an award-winning author of many books for adults and young readers, including the picture books *Norman, Speak!* (illustrated by Qin Leng) and *I Love You One to Ten* (illustrated by Christina Leist), and the Jasper John Dooley and Izzy series. Her middle-grade books are *Middle of Nowhere*, *A Simple Case of Angels* and *The Mostly True Story of Pudding Tat, Adventuring Cat*. She has won the Sheila Egoff Award, the Chocolate Lily Book Award and the Diamond Willow Award, among many other honors. Caroline lives in Vancouver, BC.

Middle of Nowhere

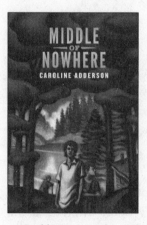

At first Curtis isn't too worried when his mother doesn't come home from her all-night job at the local gas bar. He's ten out of ten positive she'll be back, because she promised she'd never leave him again. Besides, Curtis is used to looking after himself and his five-year-old brother, Artie. For a time he manages on his own, keeping their mother's absence a secret. But when the credit card maxes out and the landlord starts pressuring for the rent, it's more than a twelve-year-old can handle.

Could Mrs. Burt, the cranky, lonely old lady who lives across the street, be the answer to their problems?

- Sheila E. Egoff Children's Literature Award, winner
- CLA Children's Book of the Year Award, finalist
- Chocolate Lily Award, nominee
- Manitoba Young Readers' Choice Award, nominee
- Junior Library Guild Selection

"Thoughtful, eventful and sharply realized, this poetic novel celebrates the resourcefulness of both the young and the old. Excellent fare."
— *Toronto Star*

"The character dynamics are just right throughout — twelve-year-old Curtis's love for Artie and grief over their missing mother are fully realized ... Adderson's success here is the subtly resilient tone (with comic notes) that will keep middle-graders going ..." — *Horn Book*

A Simple Case of Angels

Nicola's adorable little dog, June Bug, keeps getting into trouble. She steals the neighbor's turkey, yanks down the Christmas tree and destroys Mom's almost-finished giant crossword. Everyone is in a bad mood, and it looks as though the dog's days are numbered.

But then Nicola and June Bug come across a new nursing home in the neighborhood, and it feels like a Sign. They volunteer to become regular visitors at Shady Oaks, certain that June Bug's cute tricks will cheer up the elderly residents.

Will doing a good deed make up for June Bug's bad behavior?

• Junior Library Guild Selection

"Characters are gloriously quirky … Nicola navigates concepts of hell and goodness, looking for reasonable answers to ponderous questions. Though paranormal explanations are only gently hinted at, the angelic twist at the conclusion is satisfyingly appropriate and more about human goodness than evangelizing — entirely in keeping with the book." — *Kirkus Reviews*

"Though Adderson brings a light touch to some serious grown-up problems (e.g., mismanaged nursing homes) in this whimsical novel, she doesn't shy away from probing the real-world problems familiar to children. She displays a deep understanding of the complicated dynamics of childhood friendship, such as dealing with the neighborhood friend who might not be an in-school friend. Nicola's hopeful outlook and keen problem-solving skills will endear her to readers, particularly animal lovers. A sweet but never saccharine story." — *Booklist*

The Mostly True Story of Pudding Tat, Adventuring Cat

Illustrated by Stacy Innerst

Pudding Tat is born on the Willoughby Farm in 1901 — just another one of Mother Tat's many kittens. But it turns out that Pudding is anything but ordinary. He is pure white with pink eyes that, though beautiful, do not see well. He finds himself drawn to the sweet sounds of the world around him — the pattering heartbeat of a nearby mouse, the musical tinkling of a distant stream.

But before he can strike out into the wide world, he hears a voice coming from right inside his own ear, where an annoying flea has claimed Pudding as his host.

Over the next decade and a half, Pudding and his flea find themselves helping to make history — a journey over Niagara Falls in a barrel, a visit to the Pan-American Exposition on the day President McKinley is shot, a terrifying experience on the airship *America*, a voyage on the ill-fated *Titanic*, and a trip to the front lines of a World War I battlefield.

• Chocolate Lily Book Award, nominee

"Adderson not only spins a wonderful tall-tale, but the sweet relationship that develops between Pudding and his flea friend unfolds beautifully." — *Globe and Mail*

"This Forrest Gump of a cat is accompanied by an unnamed, irascible flea who acts as the cat's guide, compensating for his vision impairment ... Lovers of animal fantasy drawn to the book will find themselves taking in some history they likely never would have thought themselves interested in before." — *Kirkus Reviews*